The In Between

The In Between

MARC KLEIN

POPPY

LITTLE, BROWN AND COMPANY

New York Boston

Poppy
Hachette Book Group
1290 Avenue of the Americas, New York, NY 10104
Visit us at LBYR.com

First Edition: June 2021

Poppy is an imprint of Little, Brown and Company.
The Poppy name and logo are trademarks of Hachette Book Group, Inc.

The publisher is not responsible for websites (or their content) that are not owned by the publisher.

Library of Congress Cataloging-in-Publication Data
Names: Klein, Marc, 1969– author.
Title: The in between / Marc Klein.
Description: First edition. | New York : Poppy, an imprint of Little, Brown and Company, 2021. | Audience: Ages 14 & up. | Summary: In dual narratives, budding photographer and high school junior Tessa meets and falls in love with Skylar, and recovers from the accident that took his life, aided by his spirit.
Identifiers: LCCN 2020030148 | ISBN 9780316457712 (trade paperback) | ISBN 9780316457682 (ebook) | ISBN 9780316457705 (ebook other)
Subjects: CYAC: Love—Fiction. | Death—Fiction. | Ghosts—Fiction. | Photography—Fiction. | Family life—Fiction.
Classification: LCC PZ7.1.K6457 In 2021 | DDC [Fic]—dc23
LC record available at https://lccn.loc.gov/2020030148

ISBNs: 978-0-316-45771-2 (pbk.), 978-0-316-45768-2 (ebook)

Printed in the United States of America

LSC-C

Printing 1, 2021

In memory of Jessica Kaplan

And for Karin–
always and forever my village girl

First–Chill–then Stupor–then the letting go–

–Emily Dickinson

BLACK.

It had always been Tessa's favorite color. And not because the influencers spoke about how black was the default couture color for the rich and famous. And definitely not because the bubbleheaded fashionistas were continually asking the proverbial question: Is gray the new black, is white the new black, hell, is magenta the new black?

No, Tessa loved black because it represented absence. The absence of color, the absence of light, the absence of form. Put simply, black didn't draw attention to itself. It was invisible. And that had always been Tessa's desire in life: to stay invisible. But the black surrounding Tessa right now wasn't the invisible kind. It was a black of presence.

Where was she anyway? Last she remembered, she was getting off the city bus. It was raining outside, and with no umbrella to protect her from the downpour, Tessa was soaked from her mad dash to Skylar's house. Turning the corner, she saw his jeep backing out of the driveway, its red taillights shimmering through a wall of rain. And then...

...in an instant...

...blackness...

Tessa felt a sudden flutter of fear, disoriented by the void that had enveloped her. She was adrift in space, alone, with no stars to guide her way.

Where could she be? And more important, where was Skylar?

"I'm right here," Skylar said.

That was strange. Tessa hadn't spoken, but Skylar answered her anyway. Even stranger: She couldn't see Skylar but could sense his presence drifting beside her in this peculiar blackness with no beginning or end.

Something was weird about all this. Tessa's best guess was that she was dreaming. It was one seriously messed-up dream, but like most of them, by the time she was brushing her teeth the next morning, she'd have forgotten this craziness altogether.

Just then, a pinpoint of white light pierced the blackness. But this was no ordinary light. It was radiant and purifying, like a thousand suns of compressed love, lulling her forward, beckoning her to join with it. Tessa had never really been interested in doing drugs, but if this was what it felt like to be high, she was prepared to reconsider.

"My God, it's beautiful," Skylar said. "Let's get closer."

That was so Skylar. Always rushing toward the unknown,

not away from it. With Skylar around, Tessa felt like nothing bad could ever happen, because nothing bad ever did. So she willed herself toward the light alongside him. And that was when she began to see shapes. They were fuzzy and formless at first. But as she drifted closer, the pinpoint of light grew larger and brighter, and she saw the translucent outline of her grandma Pat. Only not the way she'd looked when she was suffering in bed those last days of her life. Backlit like a rock star, Grandma Pat was now young and vibrant.

"Uncle Andy!" Skylar screamed.

"No," Tessa said. "It's my grandma Pat."

Somehow, they were seeing different deceased relatives. How was that possible?

"Can you hear them?" Skylar asked.

"Hear who?"

"They're saying..."

There was a long pause. And Tessa suddenly sensed something was terribly wrong.

"Tessa, they're saying...you have to go back."

"What do you mean, back? Back where?"

There was now painful regret in Skylar's voice. "They say it has to be this way. That it's not your time yet."

And then something took hold of Tessa. A force. It started pulling her away from Skylar.

"Skylar, wait!" she cried.

"I'm sorry, Tess. I love you."

Everything began receding in a fast-moving blur. Tessa screamed and willed herself to stay, but the white light grew smaller and dimmer, like a dying star in a distant galaxy...

Flickering...

...flickering...

...gone.

two
hundred
and
eleven
days
before

Tessa could sense the snow even before she opened her eyes. It was an intense, luminous brightness penetrating her eyelids, urging her to consciousness. When she finally woke, the first thing she saw was light gleaming off her "Wall of Inspiration." It was a collage of words and photos on her ceiling that served only one purpose: to make Tessa feel better about her life. There were quotes (PRESERVE YOUR BUBBLE), mundane reminders (GET OFF THE INTERNET!), arty black-and-white photos (Robert Frank, Brassaï's rain-soaked streets of Paris), and even a few sketches that Tessa had drawn before she discovered her real talent lay in photography.

Most seventeen-year-olds would be rejoicing at the sight of all that fluffy whiteness outside—it meant school was canceled. But Tessa wasn't most seventeen-year-olds. For her, school was the only escape from the strangers she lived with.

Years earlier, one after the other, Tessa's real parents had disappeared without a trace. What followed was a revolving door of foster homes. Some were better than others, but most were terrifying. As for Mel and Vickie, they were the most recent childless couple who'd taken her in. Now past the one-year mark, they were undoubtedly the best of the bunch. But even though they'd recently signed her adoption papers, Tessa still couldn't fully embrace them. That would require trust, something that didn't come easily to her.

Tessa slipped some clothes on and grabbed her vintage Minolta camera, the one that was never more than an arm's length away from her. She was halfway down the stairs when she smelled a sweet aroma drifting from the kitchen. That meant Vickie had worked the night shift and was making herself breakfast. Tessa was determined to pass the kitchen silently so as to not be seen or heard, but evidently Vickie had bionic ears.

"I made pancakes," Vickie called out.

Tessa ignored her and kept moving down the hallway. She reached into the foyer closet and grabbed her puffer jacket. Vickie appeared at the entrance to the kitchen, still dressed in her casino dealer's uniform, her shiny maroon vest buttoned snugly around her torso.

"You going somewhere?" she asked.

"Out to shoot some photos," Tessa said, slipping her arms into the sleeves of her jacket.

"Now? They haven't even cleared the streets yet."

Tessa opened the front door. "I don't want to lose the morning light."

"When you get back, maybe we should do a little college research?"

"Why? Are you thinking about going back to school?" Tessa said sarcastically.

"Be serious, Tessa. It's never too early to start applying for scholarships. You have so much potential—I don't want to see you throw your future away."

What was it about Vickie that bugged Tessa so much? Was it the suffocating friendliness? The embarrassing desperation to form a mother-daughter bond? Maybe it was just something chemical—like the way dogs sometimes lunged at each other for no discernible reason. Thankfully, Tessa had discovered that a well-chosen comeback was always the quickest way to fend off Vickie's advances.

"Vickie, you're starting to sound like a refrigerator magnet."

Vickie sighed and silently retreated back into the kitchen. Tessa felt a glimmer of guilt, but not nearly enough to apologize.

Outside, the air was crisp and motionless, the sky flooding with pale light. Tessa began to wander the forsaken streets of Margate, the tiny seaside town where she lived. With Tessa's iPhone blasting her favorite indie playlist and her camera in her hands, all that existed was the rectangular world inside her viewfinder.

She snapped dozens of pictures, but found herself particularly fascinated by cars in their driveways, buried beneath snowdrifts shaped like sand dunes. It was as if Mother Nature were attempting to erase her enemies from the planet.

She continued walking through the ankle-deep snow, eventually making it to the Douglas Avenue beach. It was misty here, the sand covered with a pristine carpet of whiteness. Tessa felt like an astronaut on an alien planet, her every step disturbing the untouched perfection of the landscape. Everywhere Tessa looked, she saw something else she wanted to photograph. The foamy, white-capped waves. The weather-beaten pier that jutted out into the ocean. And a single lifeguard stand, its legs half-sunken in a snowdrift.

Far down the shoreline, Tessa noticed a lone figure materialize from a blanket of fog, like the ghost of a drowned sailor haunting the beach. All she could make out was a fiery orange baseball cap that stood out among the plumes of grayness. This was a brave soul who, like her, saw the deserted beach as an invitation to detach from the world. She took a single photograph of the orange-capped figure before they were swallowed up by the mist.

For the first time that morning, Tessa felt discomfort. There was a cold wetness on her toes. She looked down and realized she'd forgotten to put on snow boots. The sudden discovery made her conscious that her feet were on the fast track to deep freeze. By now, she was a thirty-minute walk from home. And the streets still weren't plowed, so calling Mel to come pick her up was out of the question. Maybe something in town would be open? A coffee shop or diner. Anyplace to thaw out.

When Tessa made it to Ventnor Avenue, everything appeared lifeless. Block after block, she searched for a store to rescue her from the cold. Now her feet were going numb—not a good sign. Her last hope was the town movie theater. She knew that Sherman, the owner, lived in a room adjoining the projection booth, so there was no need for him to commute. It was a long shot, but for the survival of her toes, Tessa forged ahead into the cold rush of wind.

Every time Tessa laid eyes on the Little Art Theater, she wondered how it stayed in business. It only had fifty seats, most of them lumpy with protruding springs and worn-out fabric. And now that Sherman's wife had passed away, it was strictly a one-man operation. Sherman ran the register, sold you soggy popcorn, and, when he felt ready, threw the switch on the old rattling film projector. Despite these less-than-ideal conditions, Tessa figured Sherman could have made a decent living for himself if he simply ran the latest indie movies. Instead, he chose obscure foreign films that featured lots of nudity and old B movies starring actors no one had ever heard of. One weekend, he screened nothing but famous Hollywood bombs: *Howard the Duck*, *Battlefield Earth*, and *John Carter*—a triple feature of cinematic awfulness.

As Tessa turned the corner, she was relieved when she saw Sherman sitting in the ticket booth, counting out the register. Tessa didn't even bother glancing at the marquee to see what was playing. She walked to the window and knocked on it. "You open, Sherman?"

Sherman looked up and smiled. He knew Tessa well because she was a frequent customer. "I am for you," he said, pressing a button. The machine below him spit out a ticket, which he slid through the hole at the bottom of the window. Tessa pulled a fistful of crumpled bills from her pocket and counted them out.

"Sorry," Tessa said. "I think I'm a little short."

"It's no crime. I'm only five foot six."

Tessa smiled. "I meant short of cash."

Sherman snatched the ticket back and ripped it in half, then pushed the remaining stub beneath the box-office window. "Enjoy the show, Tessa."

The musty theater was comfortably warm and smelled of burned popcorn. Tessa took a seat in the center aisle and slipped off her coat. Best part of all? She was alone. It was like her own private screening room.

Just as the lights dimmed, the door at the back of the theater swung open. A triangle of amber light widened across the floor, swimming up the walls. Tessa saw a person's shadow float across the soiled movie screen as they entered. Usually, Tessa's reaction to company in this situation would be disappointment. When in doubt, she preferred to be by herself. But somehow, she sensed that whoever had entered the theater was a friendly presence. The stranger found their way to a seat two rows behind her and sat down.

The opening credits of the movie snapped Tessa back into focus. They were all in French, even the film's title, so she had no idea what the movie was called. The first image was stark: a naked man and woman, furiously making love on a bed. Tessa began to hear a narrator speak over the images. But oddly, when she glanced to the bottom of the screen for subtitles, there were none.

In the next scene, the same couple was frolicking on the deck of a cozy beach shack, nuzzling and kissing each other. But still, no subtitles.

She had to admit—Sherman had finally outdone himself. Not only was he running films that no one wanted to see; now he was running films that no one could understand!

Tessa called out to the projection booth. "Hey, Sherman! Where are the subtitles?"

At that moment, Tessa heard the stranger behind her get up. She assumed they were going to exit the theater and complain to Sherman. Instead, the person walked down the aisle and turned into Tessa's row.

He looked to be around the same age as her, and there was just enough light in the theater to make out his shaggy mop of chestnut hair and tall, wiry frame. He took the seat next to hers, and his smell instantly enveloped her. Woody and sweet, it embodied the perfect combination of welcoming and elusive.

Despite his benign presence, Tessa couldn't ignore the fact that this boy was a stranger. Worse still, she was totally alone with him. That meant no one could help her if he planned on doing something creepy, like flashing his privates.

You need to get up, Tess. You need to get up right now and walk out. And whatever you do, don't look back or else he'll get the wrong idea.

Tessa's hands clenched the padded armrests and she leaned forward, ready to bolt. But before she could stand, the boy spoke.

"It's called *Betty Blue*," he said. "You watch, I'll translate."

He had said it kindly, but why did it feel like a command? Tessa watched him turn his head to the screen. Then, without missing a beat, he began to whisper the dialogue out of the corner of his mouth, effortlessly translating the film from French to English.

Well, that settled it. If Tessa left now, it would be rude. No, it would be more than rude—it would be like telling the universe to go to hell. A stranger had generously offered to help her, and she was just going to blow him off? Granted, she was no expert on psychopaths, but how many of them smelled so good, you felt the urge to take a bite out of them?

For the first half hour, Tessa couldn't concentrate on the movie at all. She was too conscious of the warmth of his breath on her neck and the way he pronounced certain words. She tried to guess where he was from. Was his accent from New Jersey? New York? Over time, it didn't matter anymore, because his voice began to fuse itself to the film. And before long, Tessa found herself completely immersed in the story that was unfolding before her.

The film was a tale of obsessive love. Betty, a beautiful drifter, seduces Zorg, a hapless handyman who lives in a worn-out beach shack. As their love deepens, so do Betty's spells of self-destructive rage. After discovering she was mistaken about being pregnant, Betty sadistically gouges out her own eye and winds up in a mental hospital, catatonic. In a final act of love, Zorg suffocates Betty beneath a pillow, bringing the tale to an appropriately French conclusion.

Nearly three hours after the film started, the credits began to roll. Tessa looked down and noticed her fingers clutching her translator's arm.

"Gah! Sorry!" Tessa said, abruptly releasing her grip. "How long was I doing that?"

"I don't know," the boy replied. "I lost feeling about an hour ago."

She felt hopelessly embarrassed. "How come you didn't say anything?"

"I don't know, I just assumed you were soothing me. It's a very depressing movie."

"It's a love story," Tessa said matter-of-factly.

He frowned. "Not *all* love stories are depressing."

"The good ones are."

Seeing doubt in his expression, Tessa proceeded to prove her point. "*Romeo and Juliet, Anna Karenina, Wuthering Heights,*

The English Patient. The list goes on and on. It's always the ending of a relationship—its *demise*—that makes a love story memorable."

"What about *Pride and Prejudice*? Or *Jane Eyre*? They have happy endings," he said.

"Only because those writers chose to end their love stories prematurely, before things turned dark."

"That's an interesting way of...not admitting you're wrong."

"Oh, come on," Tessa said. "Just imagine if Leonardo DiCaprio had survived at the end of *Titanic*."

"Do I have to?"

"Jack Dawson. A jobless, penniless gambler who possessed— at best—marginal artistic talent."

"I concede his technical skill was amateurish, but he saved Rose's life!"

"Only *after* he love-bombed her and stole her away from her fiancé! And poor Rose was so hypnotized by this f-boy that she actually believed he'd deliver her a life of passion and adventure. *Pleaaasssse.* More like abject poverty and dehumanizing infidelity."

"*Titanic Two.* If you thought part one was a disaster, wait until you catch the sequel," he replied.

Tessa broke out laughing, caught off guard by his quick wit.

As the movie's credits came to an end, the theater's lights rose up. And that was when the boy's piercing green eyes revealed themselves. Tessa had never seen anything like them.

They were eyes that betrayed no hint of insecurity yet still gleamed with excitement for all the unknowns that lay ahead.

"Well, I hope my translating services were satisfactory?"

"More than satisfactory," Tessa said. "If I ever become the ambassador to France, you're my go-to guy."

He smiled, then began to slip his arms into his vintage trench. When he rose to his feet, Tessa did, too. She followed him up the aisle, continuing the conversation.

"So how did you learn to speak French so well?" she asked.

"I didn't really have a choice," he said. "My dad's a professor of linguistics. When I was born, he started developing a new way to teach foreign languages, and I was his lab rat. By the time I was twelve, he had me fluent in French, Portuguese, Spanish, and Italian."

"You can't be serious. Do you ever get them mixed up?"

"Only when I dream. My dreams are totally chaotic. Someone will ask me a question in Spanish, but I'll answer them in French, and then they'll respond in Italian. Seriously, I kinda feel bad for my subconscious. Dreams are hard enough to figure out as it is—imagine if everyone in yours was speaking a different language."

By now, they had passed through the lobby and made it outside. Tessa loved emerging from a movie theater into the bright light of day. It felt like she had spent the past few hours secretly hiding out from reality. In front of them, Ventnor Avenue had finally awakened. The streets had been plowed, and cars were delicately navigating the icy pavement.

"That's some pretty old gear you've got there." The boy was now looking at Tessa's camera, which was slung around her shoulder. "You don't shoot digital?"

Tessa shook her head. "I get a much higher dynamic range on film. Plus, I'm addicted to the smell of the developing chemicals. The fumes make me delirious."

"Kind of like what your eyes are doing to me right now."

Her heart fluttered. Had he just said what she thought he had? The answer came when his face turned red with embarrassment.

"Crap," he said. "That came out way cheesy."

"No," she insisted but then decided to rib him. "Well, maybe a little bit?"

"I swear, it sounded perfect in my head."

"In that case, let me imagine that version...." Tessa shut her eyes, took a few deep breaths for dramatic effect, then popped them open.

"Still bad?" he asked.

"Kinda."

They both laughed. Behind them, Sherman had returned to the ticket booth and was staring at them. This private little moment was no longer just theirs.

"Well, I should probably, you know—" He raised his thumb and pointed over his shoulder, indicating it was time to go.

"Yeah. Me too," Tessa said quickly. She immediately worried her response was too eager, an obvious attempt to disguise her disappointment.

"Thanks for letting me whisper into your ear for three hours."

"Anytime."

With that, the tall boy with the greenest eyes Tessa had ever seen waved goodbye. She watched him head down the sidewalk, making tracks in the snow. Each step he took away from her made something inside Tessa fade a little bit—like a candle's flame getting dimmer and dimmer until all that was left was a curly wisp of smoke.

"Skylar."

She was surprised to see him poking his head out from behind the corner store at the end of the block.

"My name. It's Skylar."

"I'm Tessa."

"Maybe I'll see you here again?"

"Yeah. I mean . . . I'd like that," Tessa said.

And then he was gone.

Tessa stood in place for a few moments, attempting to process the rush of emotions she felt. Euphoria came first, a lightness that traveled through her body and threatened to lift her off the sidewalk. But this wonderful feeling was quickly undermined by a familiar sense of self-doubt. *Did I say the right thing? Did I look okay? Did he really like me or was he just being friendly?*

At that moment, Tessa felt an unconscious absence around her body. Her jacket. She'd been so consumed by this wonderful stranger, she'd left it back in the theater.

Inside, Tessa found her puffer and moved back up the aisle.

But something caught the corner of her eye. It was under the seat Skylar had first taken before he sat next to her. She walked down the row, kneeled, and slipped her hand into the shadow beneath the seat. Her fingers took hold of something and pulled it out. When it hit the light, she wasn't surprised at all. She now realized that the universe had wanted her and Skylar to meet that day. It had failed the first time, that morning on the beach, but had succeeded the second.

Because lying in the palm of Tessa's hand was an orange baseball cap.

two

hundred

and

eleven

days

before

Shannon Yeo may have been the least-exceptional junior attending Atlantic City High School. In no particular order, she was obsessed with: her hair, wearing the trendiest clothes, masturbation jokes, memorizing the lyrics to Drake songs, finding the perfect face moisturizer, the secret ingredient to her favorite low-fat cupcake (was it really chalk?), and spending Saturday nights with drunken jocks in the hope that one of them would make a move on her before he barfed himself unconscious.

For all these reasons and more, Shannon should have been the last person on earth who Tessa would have enjoyed hanging out with. But in a sublime display of cosmic ridiculousness, Shannon had been Tessa's best friend since they were twelve years old.

Shannon had arrived in Margate in the middle of the school year, transplanted by her parents from South Korea. Her father, a renowned plastic surgeon, had made a clear statement when he purchased the most expensive house on Bayshore Drive— then razed it to make room for an even bigger monstrosity.

On Shannon's first morning in her new middle school, she had taken the empty desk next to Tessa and immediately behaved as though they'd been best friends forever. "I'm Shannon," she'd said, her eyebrows arched like crescent moons. "I'd like to apologize now for talking too much. It's an issue I'm working on."

True to her warning, from that moment on, Shannon's mouth never stopped moving. It was like her voice box was powered by nuclear fuel. And it wasn't just during class that she subjected Tessa to her opinions on all things mundane. There was lunchtime. Bathroom breaks. The bus ride to and from school. Even on weekends, Shannon showed up unannounced at Tessa's foster homes for playdates. But the truth was, Shannon didn't need to work so hard. She was Tessa's only friend.

Tessa tried to build up the nerve to explain to Shannon that she wanted to be alone, that she actually *preferred* to be alone. But she could never manage the words. Too many times in her own life, Tessa had felt the sting of rejection. She'd rather dissolve in acid than inflict on others what she herself had endured.

But then, as the two girls grew up together, something miraculous happened. Through sheer grit and determination,

Shannon had turned them into inseparable best friends. True, they still didn't have much in common. Shannon shopped in boutiques with pretentious names; Tessa bought everything in musty thrift shops. Shannon yearned to be noticed; Tessa was desperate to evaporate. Shannon dragged Tessa to nail salons; Tessa took Shannon to obscure art exhibits. It was a match made in opposites heaven. But when the shit hit the fan, did it matter if your bestie preferred Nicholas Sparks to Maya Angelou? What mattered most was loyalty. Someone you could count on. Someone who'd never leave you high and dry.

Maybe that was why the moment Tessa emerged from the theater holding the orange baseball hat, her feet took her to the place they knew she needed to be: Shannon's house.

When the front door swung open, Tessa was met by Shannon's mother, whose face was always pinched in a state of concern.

"You look blue, Tessa. Where are your snow boots?" she asked.

"I really need to see Shannon, is she home?"

"I'm afraid she's sick. Some kind of infection in her throat."

"Jesus, Mom, I'm fine!"

Tessa glanced up the stairs and saw her best friend in faded sweats, looking dehydrated and pasty.

"She's contagious," Shannon's mom warned.

But Tessa didn't care about her respiratory health. She pushed past Shannon's mom, bounded up the steps, and threw Shannon a look that said, *Best friend needed ASAP.*

Tessa barreled into her friend's bedroom and was enveloped by a smell that could only be described as "sick person"—a combination of sweat, NyQuil, and scrambled eggs. She leaped onto Shannon's bed, directly into the eye of the virus. Shannon shut the door behind her and climbed onto the bed after her.

"Jesus. You look like you're ready to burst out into song and dance," Shannon said.

"The thing is," Tessa said, "I think I just found my true."

It took Tessa an hour to debrief Shannon on the morning's dramatic events. As always, Shannon was the absolute perfect audience. She laughed at all the right moments, gripped her chest when the story turned touching, frantically circled her hands when she wanted Tessa to speed things up, and grew indignant when she realized the ending of the story was a downer.

"That's it? He didn't ask for your phone number? He just gave you his name? Like, *Bond, James Bond*?"

"He also left me his hat," Tessa said as she waved it around. "At least subconsciously."

"What does *P* on the hat stand for?"

"No clue."

"Okay, I totally hate him," Shannon said.

"You have to help me find him," Tessa said. "Stat."

"Look at you—you're totally boy crazy. Now maybe you'll stop criticizing me when I flip my shit for a dude."

They spent the next two hours on Shannon's laptop, conducting an extensive internet search for anything Skylar. Thanks to years of obsessing over dozens of boys, Shannon was an absolute master at cyber stalking. "Facebook and Twitter are for amateurs," she said as she tried to find a profile of Skylar on those sites. No luck.

Next, she tried some obscure search engines that were specifically designed to help glean information about people's lives. When nothing came of it, Tessa wondered if Skylar would become one of those countless strangers who she was destined to meet but never see again.

Eventually, after finding some sites that offered public records for a fee, Shannon was forced to pull out the big guns: her credit card. Fifty dollars later, they managed to locate only three Skylars: one deceased, one retiree, and one Iraq war vet, current whereabouts unknown.

"He must have lied about his name," Shannon said.

"No way. He's not that kind of guy. If you met him, you'd know."

"It's totally weird," Shannon said. "I've never met anyone who doesn't have some kind of social media presence. Especially someone our age." She stuffed a nasal inhaler up her nose and sucked in some air.

"I think it's kinda cool," Tessa said. "He's a throwback. Like me. The last thing I'd want to find are selfies of him and his drunk buddies with red Solo cups in their hands."

"Maybe you imagined the whole thing?" Shannon offered. "Your raging adolescent hormones generated the perfect manic pixie dream boy?"

"My hormones don't speak French."

"Well, I guess the only thing left to do is develop the photos," Shannon said. "Maybe there's a clue in the photo you took of him?"

The photos! Holy hell, in all the excitement, Tessa had forgotten that inside her jacket pocket was a roll of film with the image of Skylar on the beach. She vaguely remembered he was wearing a hoodie beneath his jacket, and there was some writing on it. Could it be the name of his high school or the town he came from?

Ten minutes later, Tessa was home, developing the photos. When she'd first moved in with Mel and Vickie, Tessa persuaded them to let her convert the attic into a darkroom in exchange for the promise that if her chemicals burned the house down, she'd be stuck with a lifetime of bills and an eternity of guilt.

Over the past year, her photo supplies consumed an ever-increasing amount of her allowance and savings. Still, she defied the push to go digital. For Tessa, spending hours altering and manipulating images on a computer was just another lie in a world of lies. Wasn't the point of art to expose the truth?

That morning, she'd taken three rolls of film—with thirty-six photos on each one—but along the way had lost track of which roll had which photos on them.

Contact sheet after contact sheet materialized before her eyes in the tray of chemicals below her. Rows of tiny images appeared, a photographic reenactment of her entire morning—the barren streets, the snow-covered cars. Each successive roll took her one step closer to the beach, one step closer to the moment she'd first spotted Skylar in the orange hat. Finally, as if the whole day had been conceived by a suspense author, Tessa realized that the last undeveloped roll had the photo of Skylar on it.

Once again, Tessa switched off the light. In total darkness now, she used the can opener to crack the rim of the film canister, then spooled the undeveloped stock onto the tank reel.

Suddenly, the attic door swung open. A blanket of light swam up the stairs, quickly splashing over Tessa's hands, bathing the undeveloped film in a yellow glow. *Shit!* She'd been so excited to develop the film, she'd forgotten to lock the door.

"NO!" Tessa shrieked. "I'm developing!" She pulled the film to her stomach and crouched over, desperate to shield it from overexposing.

"Dinner's in ten minutes," her foster dad, Mel, called out, totally unaware of what he'd just done. He closed the door, and the room went dark again.

But it didn't matter. Whatever clues may have been on that roll of film had just been bleached into nothingness.

Skylar had entered Tessa's life by appearing out of a fog, and he had departed by disappearing back into one.

And now it seemed clear he intended to stay there.

four
days
after

SOUNDS PIERCED THE DARKNESS.

Beeping sounds, gurgling sounds, suction sounds, the hissing of oxygen, and random outbursts of cackling laughter. There were also Mel's and Vickie's voices, speaking to each other in hushed, anxious tones. What were they saying? Who were they talking to? It was a baffling symphony of noise, produced by an orchestra whose players Tessa could not see.

As the days and nights bled into one another, Tessa began to regain sensation. At one point, someone intentionally jabbed a sharp pin into the heel of her foot, just to see if she felt it. Her leg jerked back in pain. *Yes, I can feel it!*

But worse than the condition of her body was the state of her mind. Tessa's memory was, to put it mildly, mush. She did have a vague recollection of her strange experience with

Skylar inside the tunnel of light, but everything prior to that was a blank. Even now, as Tessa's awareness grew, she still couldn't puzzle together where she was or what was causing the constant ache in the center of her chest.

When Tessa's eyes finally opened from the haze of medication, she found herself in a colorless hospital room. Blazing sunshine was streaming through the windows, warming her face. She was lying on her side, and the first thing she saw was a man with dark skin and even darker hair. He was standing at her bedside, dressed in a crisp white coat. Upon seeing Tessa awake, he introduced himself as Dr. Nagash. He began asking Tessa questions, but her throat was too dry to speak.

"Nod if you can feel this," he said while tapping her kneecaps with a rubber-headed hammer. Tessa nodded.

"Do you remember your name?" he asked.

She did. But when Tessa attempted to utter it, only gibberish came out of her mouth. She felt frightened and confused, so she nodded again.

"Tessa, you've been in a very bad car accident. You've had some blunt trauma to your body, including your heart," he said. "We were forced to operate and repair it. Now that you're awake, it's likely you'll start to feel some discomfort in your chest and breastbone. The good news is, you're over the hump now."

A friendly nurse who smelled of floral perfume leaned in. "We've called your parents. They're on their way."

But Tessa didn't care about Mel or Vickie. And she didn't

care that her body was a mangled wreck of wounds. All she cared about was Skylar. Where *was* he?

Tessa felt like a baby attempting to speak for the first time. Finally, she croaked out a single word, posed as a question to the doctor: "Skylar?"

Dr. Nagash's expression, honed by years of delivering bad news, turned grave. "Skylar was in the accident, too. He was injured severely."

"Is he here?" Tessa asked, her voice faint and hoarse. "In the...hospital?"

"Tessa, he didn't make it to the hospital. Skylar died at the scene of the accident. I'm terribly sorry."

Every cell in Tessa's body began to revolt at the same time. She tried to scream, but all that escaped were primal shrieks of disbelief. She didn't have enough energy to weep, but tears formed in her eyes anyway. The nurse quickly injected something into her IV bag. Calmness spread through her body like liquid Zen.

Dr. Nagash tried to comfort Tessa. He assured her they had people in the hospital who would help her get over the grief. That she was still young and had her whole life ahead of her. But how could the rest of her life ever match the 211 days she loved a green-eyed boy named Skylar?

fourteen
days
after

CRYING HELPED. NOT A LOT. IT WASN'T A PERMANENT SOLUTION, but a good cry could temporarily ease Tessa's grief—and finding private places in the hospital where she could break down became a matter of survival.

The stairwell behind the neonatal unit was a good location. So was the interfaith chapel on the ground floor, though the smell of frankincense made her queasy. But the place Tessa liked to cry most was just a few short steps from her bed—the bathroom.

Tessa had a myriad of fractures and contusions. But only one of her injuries was life-threatening—her heart. It was literally broken. The car accident was so violent that it had ruptured her pericardium, the sac of fluid that surrounds the human heart. Her surgeon, Dr. Nagash, told her the fact she'd survived this traumatic injury was more than a miracle. It was unheard of—the kind of freakish outcome that wound up in medical textbooks. Naturally, this led many of the hospital's doctors to make unannounced visits in order to see the "miracle girl" for themselves. After studying her chart, they'd make eye-rolling pronouncements like "I guess heaven wasn't ready for you yet" and "You've been given a second chance, make the most of it!"

Mel and Vickie visited as often as they could. During the week, they came separately, alternating while the other worked his or her shift at the casino. On the weekends, they'd come together, usually bringing takeout because Tessa hated the hospital food.

Not surprisingly, Mel and Vickie were processing the accident in different ways. Now that Tessa was out of the woods, Mel became fixated on the impending hospital bill. "You watch," he said. "The insurance company is gonna fight us for every goddamned charge."

Vickie was preoccupied, too, but for a different reason. Prior to the accident, she and Tessa had been making real progress on their relationship. But now Vickie seemed aware that Skylar's death might mean a step backward for them. As a result, she began acting totally self-conscious, choosing her words delicately, as if fearful of setting Tessa off.

Shannon visited, too, late at night, always after visiting hours. Somehow, she'd figured out a way to sneak past the downstairs security guard. Maybe she was flirting with him?

Once safely in the hospital room, Shannon would shut the door, climb into Tessa's bed, and update her friend on the latest school gossip. She was, as always, a gift from the gods.

After two weeks, the dreams began. At first, they were mundane, just a tapestry of narratives that Tessa couldn't recall the next morning. And despite her obsessive yearning to see Skylar again, he never appeared in any of them. But then, as her physicians began weaning Tessa off her pain meds, the dreams changed. It was like her brain had switched from lo-fi to hi-fi. Everything seemed brighter, more colorful, more real. Even better, Skylar began to make fleeting cameos.

Night after night, Tessa's dreams escalated in intensity—and her interactions with Skylar became more lifelike. In her most recent one, Skylar appeared at Tessa's bedside, wearing a hospital gown. It was like Skylar hadn't died at all; he'd simply injured himself and was recovering in another room down the hall.

"You're alive," Tessa said, her eyes filling with joyful tears.

"Come on, I want to show you something."

He pulled her out of bed, then tugged her through the dimly lit hallway and up the stairwell. But he was moving too fast for her. She needed to catch her breath.

"Give me a second," she said.

"No time," Skylar said. He bent down and offered his back for her to climb onto. He carried her up the stairs, and with each step, she could feel his muscles bulging and contracting inside her embrace.

Finally, Skylar pushed through an exit door and they emerged onto the hospital's roof. It had been weeks since Tessa had felt the rush of fresh air on her face.

He carried her to the edge of the building and lowered her to the gravelly rooftop. They were ten stories up now, the nighttime cityscape sparkling beneath them. Skylar pointed to an enormous harvest moon. It was in the process of setting, its face half-buried beneath the horizon. The sky above was transforming before her eyes, a starburst of colors the likes of which Tessa had never seen.

"Come quick," Skylar said as he led her to the opposite side of the roof, the side facing the ocean. Once again, he pointed to the horizon, where a shimmer of sunlight was spreading up across the sky, spraying golden light onto Tessa's face.

It was a sensory phantasmagoria. The coldness of the setting moon, the warmth of the rising sun, and the sky above an explosion of pinks, yellows, and reds. From behind, Tessa felt Skylar scoop up her hair and lift it away from her neck. He pressed his lips to her exposed skin and she trembled, his touch rushing through every nerve in her body. Then she heard him whisper softly, "I'm still here, Tess."

Tessa jolted awake, looking around in shocked confusion. When she recognized the familiar, colorless walls of her hospital room, the euphoria of her dream evaporated, replaced by a deep cavity of anguish. Tears sprang from her eyes.

Just then, Tessa's favorite nurse, Jasmine, entered the room. Jasmine, who hailed from the Bahamas, had been named appropriately. Whenever she walked into Tessa's room, an enticing floral scent preceded her, and it lingered long after she left.

"Bad dream?" she asked.

"Who said it was bad?" Tessa replied.

"You called out his name."

Tessa reached for some tissues to dry her eyes, but the box was empty.

"It's called a visitation dream," Jasmine said, pulling a fresh box from the cupboard. "We see lots of them here. It's nothing to worry about, it's all part of the grieving process. A way that your subconscious adjusts to the loss."

"This was no regular dream, Jazz. This was like hi-def virtual reality. It felt like Skylar was here. Like he was visiting me."

"Mm," Jasmine said, clearly dubious. "I bet Doris would love to hear about that."

"Doris?"

"Cancer patient in room 406. She's had a rough year, but she's hangin' in. She claims she's writing a book about the afterlife."

Tessa raised a skeptical eyebrow. "Thanks, but I'll pass."

Jasmine chuckled. "I hear you. The other day, she offered to read my aura. I politely declined."

It was then that Tessa noticed that Jasmine was holding a

plastic bag in her arms. It was stuffed with folded clothes and vacuum sealed. She held it out for Tessa.

"What is it?"

"Your belongings from the crash," Jasmine answered. "The police returned them this morning."

"They closed the accident report? *Already?*"

"The toxicology tests indicated that neither Skylar nor the other driver had drugs or alcohol in their system. That's usually the end of it."

"They never even interviewed me," Tessa said mournfully.

"I thought you said you didn't remember anything about that night?"

That wasn't exactly true. Tessa remembered *some* things. The torrents of rain. The rivers of water rushing around her ankles as she sprinted to Skylar's house. The taillights of his jeep as he backed out of the driveway. And a broken streetlight, its bulb flickering and buzzing like a strobe. But after that, a total blank—as if the last pages of a mystery novel had been torn out by a sadistic reader, leaving the next reader unable to learn the identity of the killer.

"The fact is, you may never fully recover your memory of that night," Jasmine said. "And that's probably for the best." She patted Tessa's shoulder and walked out of the room.

Tessa glanced down at the bag. The outside read MARGATE CITY POLICE DEPARTMENT—EVIDENCE. Beneath it, someone had used a Sharpie to scribble Tessa's name, the case number, and the date of her accident. It was beyond laughable that the worst day of her life could be reduced to just a few letters and numerals.

Tessa tore along the perforated top and pulled the bag open. It released a puff of stale air. She began to dig through its contents. There were a few articles of clothing—her jeans, her T-shirt, and her canvas sneakers, which were stained with droplets of blood. There was also Skylar's orange baseball hat, now torn and soiled. And finally, there was Tessa's iPhone, which looked like it had been tenderized by an industrial meat grinder. Its black screen was shattered, its body warped like a Pringles potato chip. Despite its mangled condition, Tessa pressed the *Power* button anyway. Not surprisingly, the device refused to come to life.

Her iPhone, like Skylar, was dead.

sixteen
days
after

"DEEP BREATHS, TESSA. IN AND OUT."

She was sitting in a cramped examination room. Across from her, Mel and Vickie were side by side on a pair of chairs, playing the roles of concerned mom and dad. There were only so many expressions of worry that a person's face could exhibit, and after weeks of sustained doctor consults, Vickie and Mel had mastered every single one.

Dr. Nagash was examining Tessa, sliding the cold disk of the stethoscope across the bare skin of her chest. A jagged row of stitches bisected her breastbone, running from the bottom of her neck to the top of her stomach. Considering the size and location of the scar, Tessa would now have a legit excuse to never wear a bikini again, and that was fine with her. Tessa loathed bikinis. They made her feel maniacally self-conscious. But she wore them anyway. There was only so much peer pressure a girl could defy.

Each time Tessa inhaled, she winced as the nerves, bones, and cartilage inside her chest protested. She yearned for the early days of her recovery, when the morphine was flowing freely and she could quickly hit the *Mute* button on her pain.

Dr. Nagash yanked the stethoscope from his ears and spun in his chair, glancing at Tessa's latest CT scan on the monitor.

"I'm very encouraged, Tessa. Your heart muscle's healing nicely."

He pointed at a swirling, shifting blur of incomprehensible shapes and colors. "You can see right here, your left ventricle's functioning quite well, despite the tear."

Vickie released an audible sigh of relief. "Finally some good news."

"No doubt about it, she's a lucky girl," the doctor said. "Nine out of ten with this same injury die on my table."

"I *did* die," Tessa insisted. "The paramedics said my heart stopped for two minutes."

"That's true," Mel said. "Plus, she saw the white light. And had hallucinations."

Tessa felt irritated. She should have never told them about the tunnel of light. "They *weren't* hallucinations, Mel."

"You saw your dead grandma," he said.

Dr. Nagash chimed in. "It's called an NDE, a near-death experience. When the human body suffers severe traumatic insult, the hypothalamus floods the brain with pain-relieving opiates known as endorphins that can create aural and visual disturbances."

"So everything she saw and felt—?" Mel asked.

"Is a common neurobiological process. Absolutely nothing to worry about."

Somehow, Dr. Nagash had just reduced the most epic sensory experience of Tessa's life into a chemical equation. But how could a row of letters and numbers explain the golden-white light and the overwhelming perfection she'd felt as it enveloped her? Like it or not, no one would ever understand what Tessa had gone through. It would have to remain one of those experiences in life that was all her own.

"So when can we take her home?" Vickie asked.

"End of the week. By then I'll have run out of reasons to keep her here."

Vickie took Tessa's hand, squeezing it. But Tessa quickly pulled it away. She never liked when Vickie touched her, and she liked it even less now that her body was a gigantic wound. She saw Vickie's expression change, the rejection on her face impossible not to see.

"I want to warn you guys," Dr. Nagash said. "Tessa needs to be extremely careful these next few weeks. Her heart's still in the early phases of healing. Too much exertion or stress and she could rupture the repair. And I don't need to tell you—an acute hemorrhage would almost certainly kill her."

Dr. Nagash looked into Tessa's eyes, delivering his words with grave seriousness. "Any chest pains or shortness of breath, you stop what you're doing and call 911 immediately. Is that understood?"

one
hundred
and
fifteen
days
before

A MACHINE THAT COULD TEST DNA WOULD BE A GOOD START.

Tessa had Skylar's baseball hat and figured she could swab it for his sweat—or, if she got lucky, extract a hair fiber. Next, she'd need to access the FBI's database. Adam Zolot was Atlantic City High School's resident computer hacker. There were rumors he'd broken into Amazon's server and gotten himself free stuff for life. Tessa had no doubt Adam could use his skills to access the FBI mainframe in exchange for a couple of bucks and a little bit of flirting. If the stars were in alignment, she'd find out Skylar's last name, his phone number, and where he lived. Then she could fabricate an excuse to wander near his house one afternoon and "accidentally" bump into him when he was coming home from school. This time, though, she'd make it way more obvious that she was interested in him. She'd be totally clever and say super-witty stuff. And Skylar would be so impressed that he'd ask her to do something adventurous, like go on a trip to Paris or—

Jesus, Tessa, you need to stop! You've been running these crazy scenarios in your head for three months. Just accept it: You're never going to see him again.

It was Wednesday afternoon, and Tessa was in the back of Mr. Duffy's photography class. Mr. Duffy, a sandy-haired hippie with a penchant for paisley ties, was at the front of the classroom, critiquing another student's photo. But Tessa had already tuned him out.

She had spent the weeks following her encounter with Skylar in a state of suspended animation. Well, maybe not suspended, because she *did* try everything possible to locate Skylar, starting with the place she'd first seen him. Every weekend, she'd bring her camera to the beach and wander around taking photos, her eyes fruitlessly tracing the shoreline for his reappearance. She'd also spent countless days and nights at the Little Art Theater, sometimes watching the same film twice, hoping to cross paths with Skylar again. But despite her best efforts, the boy with the green eyes remained maddeningly elusive.

"All right, Tessa," Mr. Duffy said. "You're next."

Shit. It was time to present her photo. Tessa hated doing this. She only shared her work when she absolutely had no choice, which pretty much meant in class or when Mel refused to give her money unless he got a peek at what she was up to.

It wasn't that Tessa believed she was talentless. She knew she was the best photographer in her class, most likely the best in the school. But she also knew that every other school in the world had a "best," which meant thousands of kids were out there with equal or more talent. What were the odds that her work stood out from theirs?

Tessa walked to the front of the class. She slipped her photo out of its Mylar sheath and placed it onto the easel. She cleared her throat.

"I took it back in February," Tessa said nervously. "The day after the blizzard."

She stepped away from her photo to let the class see it. Like always, it was black and white, because Tessa believed that color drained the poetry from images. The picture was of a tall, perfectly symmetrical tree, dusted with snow. Looking at it now, in front of the class, Tessa noticed all its flaws. Wrong lens, wrong angle, too much contrast, not enough foreground. It was like looking in the mirror and feeling a strange pride that you could identify your physical imperfections.

Danny Karsevar, the class's resident comedian-in-training, was the first to comment. "That's how you spent your snow day?" he asked. "Taking pictures of *trees*?"

A ripple of laughter shot through the room. It made Tessa feel deeply uncomfortable. She hated being the center of attention. A surge of anger rose inside her, and she snapped back, "It's not a tree, asshat. It's a cell-phone tower *disguised* as a tree."

When Tessa told the class what they were really looking

at, she was met with surprised silence. Some of the students leaned in closer to confirm what Tessa had just told them.

"So it's an allegory?" Mr. Duffy asked.

"Exactly," Tessa replied. "For the artificiality of modern life. I find it disturbing that nature is insidiously being coopted by technology."

Gerald Chapman offered an enthusiastic opinion. "I think it's lit," he declared. "Tessa always notices stuff no one else does." Naturally, Gerald was being charitable; he'd been crushing on Tessa since the seventh grade.

Seeing a quick chance to score points, Danny pounced. "Forget it, bruh. Flattery ain't gonna get you a handy."

This time, the entire class broke into laughter, but they were interrupted by the bell. The students collected their bags and flooded out into the hallways.

As Tessa slipped her photo back into the plastic wrap, Mr. Duffy appeared behind her. "It's a lovely photo, Tessa. Your technical skills have taken a huge leap this year."

"I guess," Tessa answered without a trace of enthusiasm.

"I know it's a little premature, since you're still a junior," he said. "But an old friend of mine is on the admissions board of RISD. If you want, I could put in a good word for you?"

The Rhode Island School of Design? The best art school in the country? Yeah, right. She'd have a better chance of getting hit by lightning while on her way to cash a winning lottery ticket.

"Thanks," Tessa said. "But my work's really not on that level yet."

"Oh? What do you feel is missing?"

Tessa considered his question for a moment. "A point of view, I guess. Something to say that's uniquely my own."

Mr. Duffy nodded, crossing his arms. "Well, there is one thing that's conspicuously absent from all your photos."

"I know," Tessa said. "Color."

"No. *People.*"

No. That couldn't be true. She took pictures of...

Wait a second...he was right. Tessa took photos of places and environments, of empty beaches and deserted city streets. But she never put people—even people she knew—inside the rectangle of her viewfinder.

"You know, Sally Mann once said, before you find your voice, you have to find a subject you love.... What, or who, do you love, Tessa?"

Tessa realized she could not answer his question.

The city bus was overflowing with students, and the noise was close to unbearable. Tessa sat in a window seat, watching Ventnor Avenue stream by outside.

"So? What do you think?"

Tessa turned. Shannon was sitting next to her, holding up her iPad, which displayed a "build your own BMW" webpage.

"Red?" Tessa asked.

"Gaudy colors are totally on trend."

"I think you're taking advantage of your dad's generosity."

"Hell yeah! Asian dads are *putty* in your hands if you get straight As. And so far, this semester is a lock."

"Straight As? Isn't that a little ambitious for someone who's never gotten more than a C? He could buy you a pre-owned car for half the price."

Shannon flashed a face of disgust. "A hand-me-down vehicle? Okay, now you're triggering me."

Tessa laughed. It was the thing she loved most about Shannon—her unabashed displays of shallowness. Even after all these years, Tessa wasn't sure when Shannon was behaving like an actual diva—or when she was ironically mocking her privileged life as the daughter of a successful plastic surgeon. It was this guessing game that kept Tessa inexorably drawn to Shannon.

"'Sup, Tess."

Tessa looked up and saw Cortez Cole hovering above her, arm hooked around a silver pole. Cortez was athletic and adorable, with sky-blue eyes and soft blond hair that looked like it was regularly rinsed in Woolite. He carried himself like his family had a lot of money, because they did—with a ritzy house on the bay to prove it.

"You got plans this weekend?" he asked casually.

When Cortez spoke to girls (and some boys), he stirred something inside them. It was a biological fact they had no control over—like digesting food or perspiring when you get hot. And Tessa hated to admit that she, too, found Cortez sexy. But that didn't mean she had to fawn over him like every girl in school. Instead, Tessa made a conscious effort to treat Cortez as though he were inconsequential. His ego was big enough already.

"Why do you ask?" Tessa said, trying to look more annoyed than she was.

Before Cortez could respond, Shannon inserted herself into the conversation. "As it happens, I work as Tessa's full-time scheduling assistant. Thus, I can say with absolute authority that she most definitely does not have plans this weekend."

Cortez continued as though Shannon hadn't spoken. "The last row of the season is Saturday. And I was wondering if you'd come up to Cooper River and take some photos?"

"Of?" Tessa asked.

"Who else? Your daddy! It's my final high school row and I want some snaps of me kicking ass for posterity. It'll be like your graduation gift to me."

My God, his arrogance was such a turnoff.

"Sorry," Tessa said. "Sports photography isn't my thing. Maybe you can strap a selfie stick to your forehead and photograph yourself?"

But Shannon couldn't help herself. "Actually, I'm on the yearbook committee and we're dangerously low on sports shots. So I say yes, we'll be there."

"We?" Tessa asked.

"Yup. I'll join as your photo assistant."

Unreal. Shannon *always* had an agenda. And it had nothing to do with the yearbook committee and everything to do with Cortez's rowing partner, Judd, whom Shannon had been obsessed with since, well, forever.

In theory, Tessa had a choice. She *could* say no. But then Shannon would make Tessa's life a living hell, accusing her of being selfish and a crappy friend. Shannon would always end her diatribes with a good old-fashioned guilt trip: *If the circumstances were reversed, I'd do it for you in a heartbeat.*

So, no. Tessa really didn't have a choice. She *had* to play wing-girl for her bestie.

"Fine," Tessa blurted.

"Right on," Cortez said. "First race starts at six thirty. See you then."

As Cortez slipped back into the crowd, Shannon appeared horrified and quickly called out to him. "In the morning?"

Still frantic, Shannon turned back to Tessa. "He didn't mean *morning*, did he?"

Shannon insisted they get off two stops early so they could shop on Ventnor Avenue. But Tessa was still pissed off about what had gone down on the bus.

"What the hell was that back there?" she asked.

"What?" Shannon said, feigning ignorance. "We really *do* need photos for the yearbook. Besides, if you plan on being the next Annie Leibovitz, you can't be refusing assignments."

"I don't want to be the next Annie Leibovitz, I want to be the first Tessa Jacobs."

Shannon waved her hand dismissively. "You can make *way* more money as a fashion photographer."

"Don't act like you did it for my artistic growth. We both know you just want to hook up with Judd."

"What do you have against him?"

"Are you serious? The dude's like an eighties rom-com jock. All that's missing is some mousse in his hair and a brain between his ears."

"Okay. I admit Judd might be on the spectrum of bro douchiness. But they're the only guys worth crushing on."

"Not true. Skylar wasn't a douche."

"Figments of your imagination can't be *anything*, much less douches."

"I didn't imagine him," Tessa said, a touch of irritation in her voice.

"The guy's a ghost! Do you know how many hours I spent online trying to find evidence of his existence?"

"I never asked you to do that."

"To quote Dionne Warwick, *That's what friends are for.*"

"Want to be an even better friend? Forget Skylar. I have."

They stopped at the corner, waiting for the crosswalk light to turn green. Like a moth drawn to a flame, Tessa's eyes drifted across the street to the Little Art Theater. Sherman was in front, high atop a ladder, swapping out letters on the marquee. He spotted Tessa at the corner and read the expression on her face, which seemed to be asking: *Have you seen him?* Sherman shook his head with sympathy, silently answering her: *Sorry, no.*

Having witnessed their exchange, Shannon elbowed Tessa from behind. "Oh yeah. You've forgotten *all* about him."

one
hundred
and
twelve
days
before

THE DRIVE UP THE TURNPIKE WAS UNEVENTFUL. WHILE TESSA drove, Shannon slept in the passenger seat, a quadruple-shot latte nestled between her legs. For some reason, Tessa hadn't been able to pair her iPhone to Vickie's SUV that morning, so she listened to talk radio. Mostly married men and women seeking advice on how to solve their domestic woes. It occurred to Tessa that married people were the absolute worst advertisements for marriage.

An hour later, Tessa and Shannon were wandering around the Cooper River boathouse, passing teams of high school rowers as they stretched and warmed up for their races. They located Cortez and Judd down by the riverbank, in the middle of their pre-race ritual, rapping the Eminem song "Lose Yourself."

When the boys noticed Tessa was already taking photos of them, they began mugging for the camera, dancing and gesturing like hip-hop stars. Tessa lowered her camera in protest.

"I'm either taking unposed photos," she said, "or I'm not taking photos at all."

The boys seemed to get the message and resumed their warm-up.

Shannon was standing behind Tessa, sunglasses covering her sleepy eyes. Evidently, she was too tired to flirt with Judd—sexy banter was taxing—so she took the occasion to critique Tessa's work instead.

"Aren't you, like, too far away from them?"

"Only for my health and safety," Tessa replied.

"How do you expect to capture their esprit de corps and bonhomie?"

Tessa glared at her friend. "Maybe go a little easier on the SAT words?"

A voice on a loudspeaker cut through the air: "Pairs, ten minutes, into the water!"

Hooting and hollering, Judd leaped onto Cortez's back and they crumpled to the dirt in a heap of male adolescence.

Tessa rolled her eyes. "Ladies and gentlemen, I give you toxic masculinity."

"I'm gonna need you to put this on."

An aging jock with a round belly was holding out an orange

life vest for Tessa. She noticed several other chubby middle-aged men on the coach boat, but not one of them was wearing a life vest.

"Why only me?" Tessa inquired. "Because I'm female?"

"No. Because the rest of us are fat. And blubber floats!"

The coaches all burst into laughter. Tessa realized that when jocks aged, they didn't change in the slightest. They were still arrogant dipshits, only with less hair and wider waists.

Tessa slipped the life vest over her head. It was damp with river water and felt cold on her bare neck. The engine beneath her feet suddenly came to life, and Tessa inhaled a cloud of pungent exhaust that smelled strangely pleasant.

Shannon shouted from the shore. "I'll meet you at the finish line, Tess!"

Tessa waved to Shannon as the coach boat reversed out of the dock and made a wide arc to the starting line, where all the teams were preparing for the fifteen-hundred-meter race.

Tessa was pleased to discover that Cortez and Judd were in the lane closest to her, which meant she'd have an unimpeded view for her photos.

"READY ALL!" said a voice through a bullhorn.

Tessa raised her camera. Looking through the viewfinder, she saw Cortez and Judd seated inside their two-person shell, hands gripping their oars, legs locked and loaded. Once again, she resisted the ember of attraction she felt for Cortez. She reminded herself it was like looking at a Greek sculpture in a museum. You could admire its beauty even though it was inert, just like Cortez's personality.

And then, through the bullhorn: "ROW!"

The shells leaped out of the gate. Immediately, the engine beneath Tessa's feet whined and the boat lurched forward. Foam churned from beneath the hull as the craft quickly gained speed, catching up to the rowers, pacing alongside them so their coaches could watch and correct their technique.

Cortez and Judd were off to a good start, already a few strokes ahead of the others. Tessa focused her lens on Cortez's face, capturing his determined intensity. Next to Tessa, the coaches were shouting directions to their respective teams: *"Pump harder!" "Feel the connection!" "Thrust through the middrive!" "Thrust! Thrust!"*

As they passed the race's midpoint marker, Cortez and Judd had a comfortable lead and showed no signs of flagging. But then something appeared on the left side of Tessa's viewfinder, poking its nose into the frame. At first, it was just a blur, an unconscious distraction. But then Tessa realized it was another shell, sneaking up behind Cortez and Judd. Intrigued, Tessa swung her camera to the left and focused on two other rowers.

Two more rowers fighting to win.

But one of them, the one in the front, looked...familiar.

Actually, he didn't just look familiar—he *felt* familiar, as if he were transmitting an invisible energy that only Tessa could receive. His biceps were swelling and contracting as his body gracefully slid back and forth in the boat, his blades dipping in and out of the water with fluid perfection. It took Tessa another few seconds to register that he was wearing an orange tank top with a black letter *P* on it.

No. It's not possible. It can't be.

Tessa turned, her eyes tracing the pack of coaches on the boat with her. She noticed one of them was wearing an orange hat with a black letter *P* on it. A hat identical to the one Skylar had left in the movie theater.

"Excuse me," Tessa screamed to him. "What team are you with?"

Without averting his eyes, the coach answered, "Princeton High!"

Chest tightening, Tessa dug through her camera bag and pulled out her zoom lens. She quickly swapped it with the 50mm lens she'd been using all morning. Tessa leveled her camera and twisted the lens so she could get a closer look at the Princeton High team. At first, they were fuzzy. But then Tessa tightened the focus ring....

And that was when Skylar came into view.

Weakness coursed through Tessa's body, causing her grip on the camera to slip. It swung on its strap, striking her breastbone, causing a sharp lance of pain.

Within a few seconds, Skylar and his partner had overtaken the others. And now they were side by side with Cortez and Judd, trading the lead with every stroke.

Cortez and Judd seemed offended by the boat next to theirs, whose bow was now inching ahead of them. Tessa had never seen Cortez look so harried, so helpless. There was extra pleasure in knowing it was Skylar who was making him feel that way. Cortez and Judd were rowing as hard as they could, desperately gulping air. But they were no match for Skylar and his partner, who rushed ahead and crossed the finish line to win the race.

Shannon was seriously ticked off. "You never told me he was hot!"

"Uh, yes I did," Tessa said.

"No. You said he was *cute*. Emojis are cute. That guy is, like, tap-on-the-first-date hot!"

"Shhh!"

Tessa and Shannon were standing about twenty yards away from Skylar, gawking at him. He was on his back, sprawled on the wooden dock. He was still breathing heavily from the race and was struggling to pull his sweat-drenched tank top over his head. When he finally got it off, Shannon let out a gleeful moan.

"Good lord," she said. "He's got ab muscles I didn't know existed!"

As the seconds passed, Tessa grew more anxious. She'd fantasized about this reunion in a million different ways, but now that Skylar was in range, she wondered whether it would be best to leave him a mystery.

"Let's just go," Tessa said, turning toward the parking lot.

Shannon forcefully took hold of her. "Go? What are you, cracked? You've been obsessing about this dude for months. You can't walk away now."

"What do I even say to him?" Tessa asked.

"Hold me?"

"Be serious, Shannon!"

"Just start with something simple like . . . congrats. He won the race, didn't he?"

Tessa sighed. "Reality can never live up to our fantasies."

"Maybe so. But reality's the only place that serves froyo. Now, go be charming."

Shannon shoved Tessa forward, toward the dock. From behind, Shannon called out to her, "Can I shoot your reunion for my Insta?"

"Only if you seek a premature death."

With each step Tessa took, nervousness stirred inside her chest. *What should I say? My God, what if he doesn't remember me? What if he has a serious girlfriend?*

When Tessa finally advanced onto the dock, she stopped before Skylar's feet, hovering over him. He squinted, holding his hand up to block the blazing sun. Tessa stood in place, frozen like a statue. All she was able to muster was a single word.

"Bonjour," she said.

Upon seeing her, Skylar's face immediately brightened. It was obvious that he not only remembered Tessa but was thrilled to see her. He quickly sprang to his feet and screamed her name. "Tessa!"

But then Skylar winced, his expression transforming from joy to distress. His legs buckled beneath him and he pitched forward, surprising Tessa by landing inside her embrace. She couldn't hold him up, and they both crumpled to the dock, a tangle of limbs.

Skylar flashed an embarrassed smile. "Damn, sorry about that. After a race, my legs are like Jell-O." He struggled to his feet, steadied himself, and helped Tessa back up.

"I cannot believe you're a jock," Tessa said.

"Oh, come on, we're not so bad."

"Jocks don't speak French, Italian, Spanish, and Portuguese."

"This one does," he said.

"Well, they *definitely* don't read Jane Austen and Charlotte Brontë."

Skylar shrugged. "What can I say, I've got this weird thing for happy endings."

Tessa couldn't help but smile, relieved that he still remembered the details of their conversation. The same conversation she'd replayed in her mind dozens of times, line for line, these past three months.

Before Tessa could reply, a woman's voice shrieked out from behind them. "Now, that's what I call a finish!"

Skylar rolled his eyes. "Oh shit."

It was the kind of *oh shit* that teenagers only made when their parents were approaching. Sure enough, a few seconds later, a slim woman with blond hair and delicate features appeared behind Skylar. She enthusiastically wrapped her arms around his bare torso and bombed him with a flurry of affection.

"Jesus, Mom, can you *please* chill on the PDA?"

Skylar's mom reluctantly released her son, then noticed Tessa standing across from her, silent. After a moment, his mom's eyes widened in recognition. "Movie theater girl!"

Wait, *what*? How on earth could his mom know who she was?

"Mom, her name's Tessa."

"I don't understand," Tessa said. "How did you know . . . ?"

"The blue eyes!" she answered. "Skylar went on and on about them."

Skylar blanched in embarrassment. "Anyone see a deep, dark hole I can climb into?"

"You know, he spent weeks and weeks searching for you on the internet . . ."

"Mom!"

". . . but couldn't find a thing about you."

"That's by design," Tessa said with pride.

"See?" Skylar said. "I told you. She's old-school, like me."

A ringtone interrupted them. Skylar's mom pulled her phone from her pocket and looked at the screen. When his mom saw who was calling, her brow furrowed with unease.

"It's your father." She sighed.

"Answer it. Tell him I won," Skylar said.

But Skylar's mom hit the *Ignore* button. "You can call him later yourself." She stuffed the phone away and turned back to her son. "Are you taking the team bus home?"

"No," Skylar said. "I drove down here. I'm gonna spend the weekend with Grandpa. But first, I was gonna see if Tessa wanted to go on a date with me?"

It took all of Tessa's effort not to break out into a euphoric dance. She absolutely adored that he'd used the word *date*. It wasn't old-fashioned at all. It was a sign that he was interested and wasn't afraid to say so. But of course, Tessa couldn't let him see her excitement, so she managed a subtle, oh-so-cool shrug that seemed to say: *Sure, what the hell.*

Skylar's mom appeared puzzled. "A date? I thought kids today didn't go out on dates. I thought you—what do they call it—Hulu and hang?"

Tessa and Skylar shared a smile.

"That," Tessa answered, "comes *after* the date. And please tell your son that 'movie theater girl' would love to go on a date with him."

nineteen
days
after

ON HER FINAL NIGHT IN THE HOSPITAL, TESSA BEGAN TO FEEL A familiar sense of grief bubbling up inside. Like always, it would only be a matter of time before this bubble would burst, releasing a spasm of full-blown hysteria. It was definitely time to cry.

Tessa slipped from the covers and swung her feet to the floor. She saw Skylar's orange baseball hat sitting on the night table and had a sudden inspiration. Tonight, Tessa would bring the cap with her to the bathroom. This way, as she cried, she could touch something that he had once touched.

Locking the door, Tessa sat on the cold tile floor and slumped against the wall. Tears fell down her face, over her chin, and down her neck. She began to communicate with Skylar's hat, silently asking it to cheer her up. *Share some memories with me*, she pleaded. *Make the pain go away.*

Ever since she had found Skylar's hat in the movie theater, Tessa had tried to return it to him. But each time she offered it, he refused, insisting the universe wanted her to have it. Unconvinced, Tessa finally snuck it into Skylar's backpack when he wasn't looking. Days later, however, she found the hat in her bedroom closet, nestled between some sweatshirts. Thus began a running summer joke. Tessa would sneak the hat into Skylar's belongings—his glove compartment, his pillowcase—only to find it a few days later among her things.

"Obviously, the gods want you to have the hat," Skylar declared, a look of innocent charm on his face.

There was suddenly a soft knock on the bathroom door. The sound whisked Tessa away from her summer memories, delivering her back to the cold tile floor.

"One sec," Tessa called out. It was probably Jasmine, making sure she was okay.

Tessa rose to her feet and yanked some tissues from a box beneath the sink. She blew her nose while spying her reflection in the mirror. It was incredible what weeks of depression could do to a human face. Her eyelids were swollen, sore to the touch. She had matching black circles beneath each eye socket. But worst of all was the pastiness. All the foundation in the world couldn't bring color to her complexion.

Another knock came. This one a little louder, more insistent.

"Okay, Jazz," Tessa said. "Coming."

She swung open the bathroom door, expecting to see

Jasmine standing there. But the doorway was empty. Puzzled, Tessa peeked out into the hall, but the ward was desolate, the nurses' station unattended.

Weird. Tessa was certain she'd heard someone knock. Could she have imagined it? Not likely. Her medical team had scanned her brain multiple times and, thankfully, found no damage at all.

Ping!

The sound of a text message bounced through the air. It had been a while since Tessa heard the "ripples" ringtone she'd chosen for her text alerts.

Wait a second. A text alert? That was impossible. Her phone was trashed. Tessa spun around, her eyes drawn to her nightstand, where she'd left her mangled iPhone. Only now, its screen was glowing light blue. Somehow, it had turned on.

Upon realizing her phone had, like her, defied the odds and recovered from its injuries, Tessa anticipated hearing more pings, a flood of them actually. After all, Tessa had been in the hospital for close to three weeks. And with the exception of Shannon, Tessa had been out of touch with every acquaintance in her life. There was undoubtedly a traffic jam of phony "get well" messages piled up, waiting for Tessa to turn on her phone. Only now that her phone *was* on, the room stayed silent. No more pings.

It was just as she always suspected. Nobody gave a crap about her.

Tessa crossed the room and picked up her phone, lifting

the screen so she could read the text. A wave of shock raced through her body when she saw it was from Skylar.

Her heart surged with excitement, and immediately, she felt a series of unbearable, stabbing pains in her chest. Each time her heart thumped, she felt another eruption of pain. Dr. Nagash, it seemed, wasn't messing around. Stress didn't just mean discomfort; it meant agony. She took a few deep breaths, allowing her heartbeat to resume its normal rhythm, and thankfully, the pain tapered off.

Tessa looked back down at her phone. She realized it was likely the final message Skylar had sent her, unaware that when he pressed *Send*, his life was minutes from ending. She tapped her thumb to the cracked screen, and the text sprang open. But there was no message. Instead, she saw a square box that read *Attachment: 1 Image*.

His final communication came not in words, but as a picture.

Tessa tapped the icon with her fingertip. As the pie chart began to fill up, a photo downloaded on the screen, materializing line by line, pixel by pixel.

A misty beach...

A shack on stilts...

And Betty and Zorg, kissing on the deck of their beach shack.

BETTY BLUE!

It was a still from the first movie they had seen together. She and Skylar had often talked about the film, fantasizing about how perfect it would be to spend a week, a month, or forever in that adorable beach shack together.

Just then, from behind her, she heard Skylar's voice: "You watch, I'll translate."

A chill shot up Tessa's spine, causing her to tremble. *You watch, I'll translate?* Those were the first words he'd ever spoken to her in the movie theater. Tessa whirled around, but the room behind her was empty.

Could she be hearing things...? Imagining his voice...? No. Not possible. Because seeing was believing...and the photo of the beach shack was definitely on her screen....

But when Tessa looked back down at her phone, the image of the beach shack was gone, replaced by a dull rectangle of black.

Once again, her cell phone was dead.

twenty
days
after

"THAT'S HER, RIGHT OVER THERE."

The orderly pointed to a woman sitting in a wheelchair beside the koi pond. Tessa thanked him and walked through the garden toward the woman. It felt good to be outside in the sun, and even better to be dressed in her regular clothes.

Mel and Vickie were downstairs, signing forms and going through the bill of services. Tessa had told them that she wanted to say goodbye to a few of her doctors and nurses and that she'd meet them in the lobby in fifteen minutes. But on the way back downstairs, she'd decided to take a little detour.

The woman sitting in the wheelchair looked to be in her sixties. She was completely hairless. Her eyebrows and eyelashes were gone—and her bald head was covered with a scarf imprinted with the Puerto Rican flag. A stack of disordered papers sat on her lap, and she was writing in a frenzy, lost in a trancelike state.

"Hi," Tessa said nervously. But the woman in the wheelchair did not respond. She kept writing. So Tessa spoke louder. "Are you Doris?"

The woman finally stopped and looked up. She had soft, pale blue eyes, and her face was frightfully emaciated. "I'm gonna take a wild guess," she said. "Fifth floor? Girl with the broken heart?"

Tessa felt a swell of surprise. How did this woman know who she was? Was she psychic?

"No," Doris said, as if reading Tessa's mind. "I'm not psychic. Jasmine told me you might come looking for me. I'm terribly sorry for your loss."

"Thanks," Tessa said.

"Are your hands injured?" Doris asked.

"Excuse me?"

"In the accident. Did you hurt your hands at all?"

"No, why?"

Doris reached into a tote bag that sat on the rim of the koi pond. She removed a bottle of hot-pink nail polish and dropped it into Tessa's palm. Then Doris wiggled her fingers, indicating that Tessa had just been recruited to be her manicurist.

Amused and intrigued, Tessa pulled over a chair and began painting Doris's nails. She glanced down at the handwritten pages on Doris's lap, guessing it was the book that Jasmine had mentioned.

"So what's your book about?" Tessa asked.

"How to make the perfect grilled cheese sandwich," Doris said, then smiled broadly. "Just kidding. It's about ADCs."

"ADCs?"

"After-death communications."

Tessa hesitated, then finally asked, "So you believe dead people can—?"

"Don't use that word. They're *not* dead. They're simply disembodied spirits."

"Sorry...So you believe these...*disembodied spirits* can contact us?"

"I certainly do. Along with billions of other people from faiths that span the globe. You know, in China, they actually allow the living to marry the dead?"

"Seriously?"

"They're called *minghun*—ghost weddings. I personally haven't attended one, but I hear they're lovely affairs. Plenty of dim sum. Don't you just love dim sum? Of course, I've also interviewed dozens of people who've had their own experiences." Doris tapped the manuscript on her lap with great pride. "It turns out, the deceased can contact us in a myriad of different ways. Sometimes, we smell their cologne or perfume in the air. That's called an olfactory ADC. Other times, we hear their voices. That's an auditory ADC."

Tessa felt a rush of excitement. That was exactly what had happened the night before in her hospital room—she'd heard Skylar's voice.

Doris continued. "No matter how they communicate with us, their message is the same: *I'm still here, and your grief, like a beacon, calls me to your side.*"

"What about a phone?" Tessa asked. "Could a dead person—I mean, could a *disembodied spirit* send a message through a cell phone?"

"At the turn of the twentieth century, the number of recorded ADCs was in the hundreds. By the turn of the twenty-first century, that number was in the millions."

"Why? What happened?"

"Technology happened," Doris said. "You have to understand, the deceased exist on an entirely different vibratory frequency from ours. They're pure astral energy…."

Astral energy?

"It stands to reason they'd be able to manipulate any number of electrical devices. Computers, TVs, even your cell phone." Doris's eyes were aflame now. "Remember last year when the whole electrical grid went down?"

"That was a ghost?" Tessa asked skeptically.

"It's all in here," Doris said, lifting the papers off her lap. "Chapter eleven."

Tessa's eyes washed over Doris's childlike chicken scratch and the primitive, indecipherable sketches she had drawn. It looked like the diary of a madwoman, the kind of notebook a homicide detective uncovered among a serial killer's belongings.

"I see doubt in your eyes," Doris observed.

"No," Tessa said, trying to be sensitive but now confident this woman was a kook.

"Don't you think your boyfriend wants to see you as desperately as you want to see him?"

Tessa heard Vickie's voice call out to her. Tessa turned and saw Mel and Vickie standing in the entrance to the garden, both holding piles of paperwork. Mel looked nauseous, which likely meant the out-of-pocket charges for Tessa's care were astronomical.

"Time to go home!" Vickie said.

Tessa yelled back, "One sec!" She finished painting the final nail on Doris's hand, then slipped the wand back into the glass bottle. She screwed the cap closed and rose to her feet.

"Wait," Doris said. She pulled something from her tote bag, careful not to smudge the wet polish on her nails. She held out an old, faded book with a torn dust jacket. "Take this. It's my first book. It's a good place to start."

But Tessa was not interested in reading this wacko's book. "That's okay, I'm good. Thanks for talking to me, Doris. Be well."

As Tessa turned to leave, Doris grabbed her wrist. "Soon, you'll change your mind. Soon, your boyfriend will get better at it. His ADCs will grow more insistent....Less like a gentle touch...more like a powerful shove."

With that, Doris lifted her pen and resumed work on her manuscript.

one
hundred
and
twelve
days
before

TESSA CHANGED OUTFITS SEVEN TIMES. AND EVEN THEN, SHE
still wasn't happy. Nothing looked right, not even her favorite dress, the one that hid everything she wanted hidden and
revealed everything she wanted revealed. She finally settled
on a pair of faded blue jeans, a charcoal cashmere sweater, and
a pair of vintage strappy sandals she'd bought at a thrift store
the prior summer.

She studied her hair. Last fall, she'd styled it in a bob and
dyed it blond. Tessa liked it best when her roots started showing, forming a dark strip across the center part of her hair. But
since she'd bleached it only a few days ago, the strip wasn't
there. And it bothered her that she wasn't presenting her best
self to Skylar.

God, she *hated* when she got like this. A vanity spiral. If only she could approach her appearance with the same obsession for authenticity that she sought with her photos. Then again, could anyone blame her for feeling inadequate? Only on a desert island would a girl her age be free from the daily Instagram assault of flat bellies, round butts, and voluptuous boobs.

"Are you wearing perfume?"

Tessa spun around and saw Vickie standing in her bedroom doorway. Dammit. Why hadn't she locked her door?

"It's body lotion," Tessa answered curtly.

"You have something planned for tonight?"

Tessa sighed, realizing it would be impossible to avoid the conversation. "If you must know, I have a date."

As if on cue, Mel stepped out of the bathroom, a folded newspaper beneath his armpit. "A date?" he asked. "With a boy?"

"I don't know, Mel. I haven't undressed him yet."

The doorbell rang. *Bless you, Skylar*—literally saved by the bell.

Tessa pushed past Vickie and Mel and raced downstairs. She took a deep breath, steeling herself for the night ahead, and swung open the front door. She was surprised to find Cortez standing there, sweatpants pulled up past his ankles, his hair damp and downy.

"Yo, yo, Tess. What's crackin'?"

"Cortez? What are you doing here?"

"What do you mean? Came by to get my snaps. C'mon, you

can help me pick out the best ones." He started to enter the house, but Tessa held out her hand to stop him.

"Sorry, I don't have time right now."

"Come on, Tess. It'll only take a few minutes."

Cortez noticed Mel and Vickie at the top of the stairs, looking down at him. "What up, fams!" he said cheerfully.

"Is *he* your date?" Mel asked.

Cortez's eyes darted nervously back to Tessa. "Date? What's he talking about?"

Tessa forcefully pushed Cortez out of the doorway and down the porch steps. "Look," she said. "I haven't developed your photos yet. But I promise I'll bring the contact sheets to school on Monday, okay?"

"Contact sheets? Why can't we just look at them on your laptop?"

Oh Jesus, this was getting worse by the minute. But then, thankfully, a lifeline...

A 1980s Jeep Cherokee with its top down turned the corner and coasted down the street. Skylar was behind the wheel. He turned into Tessa's driveway and parked just inches from the back of Vickie's SUV.

Skylar climbed out of the jeep. He was wearing dark khakis and a V-neck T-shirt beneath a gray hoodie. Upon recognizing Skylar, Cortez appeared surprised. But not as surprised as Tessa was when she saw Skylar throw his arms around Cortez, giving him a friendly, robust hug. "Nice race, bro," Skylar said.

"You guys fuckin' *killed* it!" Cortez replied.

Tessa was hopelessly confused. "Wait. You guys know each other?"

"Cortez?" Skylar said. "We've been rowing against each other since freshman year. Mostly I beat him."

"Bullshit, yo! Today was a total fluke."

"Right," Skylar said. "Keep telling yourself that."

Oh God. It was a "bro" explosion. Teenage boys, overdosed on cockiness and testosterone, were attempting to one-up each other in Tessa's presence.

Always a little slow on the uptake, Cortez finally added two and two together. "Hold on," he said. "Are y'all hooking up?"

This was becoming a nightmare. Even worse, Tessa saw that Mel and Vickie were now standing behind the screen door, watching the drama unfold.

Tessa gripped Skylar's shoulder. "Can we please go?"

"Don't you want me to meet your folks?" he asked innocently.

"Some other time," Tessa said.

Skylar seemed to sense the urgency in her voice. He looked over Tessa's shoulder at Mel and Vickie and flashed them a respectful smile that said, *Chill, I'm not a serial killer.* Then he turned back to Cortez and made a fist, and they tapped knuckles.

"Peace out, brother," Skylar said.

"Word. See you on the college circuit."

Skylar placed his hand on the small of Tessa's back and led her to his jeep and into the front seat.

As they pulled out of the driveway, Tessa glanced once more at her lawn. She saw three people standing side by side, staring at her—Mel, Vickie, and Cortez. It was a trio she could have never imagined, not even in some warped alternate universe.

As Skylar sped down Ventnor Avenue, the rush of air swept Tessa's hair skyward.

"Want me to put the top up?" he asked.

"No," Tessa said. "It feels good."

She brushed the hair away from her eyes and pulled it back, tying it into a nest. She caught Skylar watching her, his gaze lingering on the exposed skin of her neck. She detected a charge of excitement in his eyes, and it made her feel sexy.

"You look amazing," he said.

"Can you say it in French?"

"*Tu as l'air fantastique.*"

"You too," she replied.

Tessa was suddenly distracted by a clinking sound. It was Skylar's key ring, swinging back and forth, jangling against the steering column. The key ring was a small plastic case that housed a color photo of two people with their arms around each other. One was Skylar, the other a beautiful blond girl.

Tessa felt queasy and couldn't stop herself from blurting out, "You don't have a girlfriend, do you?"

Skylar seemed baffled by her question. "Not since the tenth grade. Why?"

Tessa gestured to the key ring. Skylar looked down and chuckled. "That's my mom and dad when they were teenagers. They grew up down here, so we spent every summer with my mom's dad, Grandpa Mike. This was actually the jeep Grandpa bought my mom. Look, you can see it in the picture."

Tessa leaned forward and studied the photo. Skylar's parents looked to be around the same age as Tessa and Skylar. His father was cute and preppy, dressed in pleated shorts and a U2 concert T-shirt. Though not as athletic-looking as his son, he was handsome and appeared self-assured.

In contrast, Skylar's mom was 100 percent New Wave. She was wearing a pink tube top, Reebok sneakers, and a jangle of rubber bracelets on both wrists. Her hair was permed in Madonna's "Like a Virgin" style. It was hard to imagine that this trendy girl would one day grow up to be the normie, middle-aged mom who Tessa had met earlier that day.

Sure enough, the red jeep was parked behind them in the photo. It was brand-new back then, paint gleaming, tires shiny.

"They look insanely lovesick," Tessa observed.

"They were."

"*Were?*"

"*Are.* My dad's living and teaching in Oregon right now."

"That's pretty far away. Are they taking a break?"

"No, they still talk every day. They're gonna be fine."

It was obvious that Skylar didn't want to talk about his parents, so Tessa let it go.

"Hey, do me a favor?" Skylar pointed to the floor beneath her seat. "Look under your seat, there's some music there."

Tessa reached down and took hold of a padded, rectangular box. She unzipped the cover and discovered several rows of cassette tapes inside. She had seen tapes like this before, in the garage, buried among Vickie's things.

Tessa scanned the albums...New Order...Kate Bush... INXS....It was a treasure trove of 1980s alternative music.

"Okay," Tessa declared. "Your mom's my new bestie."

There was one cassette tape that drew Tessa's attention. It had tiny red hearts drawn on its spine and a list of song titles handwritten on the insert.

"Awww," Tessa said. "Your dad made her a romantic mixtape?"

"It's the best cassette in there."

"Can I put it on?"

"Sure."

Tessa opened the plastic case and pulled out the cassette. She attempted to slide it into the tape player in the jeep's dashboard, but it wouldn't fit.

Holding back a laugh, Skylar corrected her. "Other way."

Tessa blushed. "Oh crap."

"Don't worry, I won't call the eighties police."

Smirking, Tessa flipped the tape around and slipped it into

the hole in the dash. After a momentary blast of fuzz, a song Tessa had never heard began playing. It was an achingly evocative love song, and the singer's bittersweet voice stirred deep emotions inside her.

More than this, you know there's nothing...
More than this, tell me one thing...

"Who is this?" Tessa asked.

"Roxy Music. It's called 'More Than This.' Do you know them?"

"Don't think so."

They listened to the rest of the song without talking. When it finally ended, Tessa noticed that Skylar had U-turned and was now heading back in the opposite direction.

"Are you lost?" she asked.

"Not at all," he said.

"Well, where are we going?"

"Honestly? I'm so nervous right now, I have no clue."

Smitty's was a tiny clam shack situated on the bay. It was the kind of restaurant that locals worked hard to keep a secret, though not always successfully. Tessa and Skylar found an empty table on the outdoor patio, a few feet shy of the adjoining dock. They ordered a shrimp boil and two lemonades.

Fifteen minutes later, their waitress returned, lugging a steaming bucket of shrimp and potatoes, which she overturned onto the tabletop before them.

They got to work, peeling shrimp and juggling the hot spuds with their bare fingers.

"Seriously," Skylar said. "I've spent every summer of my life down here. How do I not know this place?"

"Believe it or not," Tessa said, "I stumbled on Smitty's by accident. That's actually my favorite part of taking pictures. Just wandering around and discovering places that no one else knows."

"Okay, but what drew you to this spot? Specifically?"

"The view," she answered.

Skylar looked over Tessa's shoulder to admire the marina and the tranquil bay spreading out behind it.

"Actually," Tessa said, "the *other* view."

He turned, following the direction of her finger. Across the service road sat an old, dilapidated hotel resort from the 1960s. It was a decaying carcass, battered by years of woeful neglect. Its exterior paint had long ago been blasted away by the elements, and the boarded-up windows were covered with indecipherable graffiti.

"A honeymooners' resort?" Skylar asked.

Tessa nodded. "It's unbelievably surreal inside."

"You've gone in there? Unarmed?"

Tessa smiled with pride. "I'll do anything for a great photo."

Above the main entrance, Skylar noticed a cracked neon sign with the resort's name written in florid script. "The Empyrean Hotel?" he read.

"The Empyrean is the place—"

"—where Dante met God."

Tessa lit up, impressed that Skylar knew this obscure reference.

"It's the highest of all heavens," he stressed. "A place of pure, unadulterated love."

Skylar glanced back at the resort, studying its faded grandeur. He gestured to Tessa's phone, which was sitting face-down next to her. "I'd love to see some of your photos from inside."

"I don't have any of them on my phone. I don't shoot digital, remember?"

"Okay, but... what if someone wants to see your work?"

"I don't show my work. Unless I have to. For class."

"How come?" he asked.

"Because it's not good enough."

Skylar raised an eyebrow. "I find that hard to believe."

Tessa forced a cordial smile. Over the years, she'd received numerous compliments about her photos, but nothing anyone ever said convinced her that her work was anything special. Mostly, the compliments irritated her. They were either outright lies or the words of people who knew little to nothing about photography. But now wasn't the time to debate the issue.

"Well," Skylar said, "if I can't see your photos, how about a tour?"

"Of the hotel?" Tessa asked.

"Yeah. I'd like to see it...through your eyes."

Skylar insisted on paying the bill. Then Tessa led him across the service road and around to the back of the resort, where a wooden board had been kicked in, leaving an open window frame for them to climb through.

She started the tour in the lobby. It was a massive space, with vaulted ceilings, marble floors, and varnished wooden walls, inlaid with ornate etchings of mythological lovers. A spiral staircase corkscrewed to the second level of the hotel. It appeared to float in space, seemingly held up not by columns or wires but magic. Tessa's favorite part of the lobby was located on the wall behind the check-in desk. It was a large, hand-painted heart with the words YOU ARE ENTERING THE LAND OF LOVE written inside. She had photographed the sign many times.

"*That*," Skylar said as he admired it, "is beyond awesome."

Next she led him through the dining hall. It was the size of a football field, a shadowy expanse of tables and overturned chairs. On the ceiling hung several opulent chandeliers, their dangling crystals shrouded in decades of dust.

They played Ping-Pong in the game room, using the soles of their shoes as paddles. Tessa won twenty-one to seventeen, but she sensed that Skylar had let her win.

There was a cocktail lounge, amusingly named "Cupid's Arrow." Weeds had grown through the floorboards and were crawling up the walls. Skylar plucked a single daisy from the ground and slipped it behind Tessa's ear. His touch was only a graze against her earlobe, but she felt it through her entire body.

In the ballroom, Skylar pulled a lampshade off one of the wall sconces, placed it over his head, and proceeded to dance for Tessa. She couldn't stop giggling. Skylar had memorized all the steps from an old boy-band video. Before long, Tessa leaped onstage and joined him, trying her best to match his moves.

As the tour progressed, Tessa felt an increasing desire to kiss Skylar. But unlike Shannon, she'd never made the first move with a guy. Her fear of rejection far outweighed any desire she might have. So she had no choice but to wait, all the while sending Skylar as many subtle cues as possible.

Finally, she led him into the resort's largest and fanciest room, the Eros Suite. It had mirrored ceilings, wall-to-wall shag carpets, and a four-post bed with only two posts left. But the highlight had to be the Jacuzzi. It was made of clear, thick plastic and shaped like a stemmed champagne glass. A ladder on the side allowed them to climb up and lower themselves into the tub.

With their shoulders lightly pressed against each other, they gazed up through the cracked ceiling window, watching the sky change colors from day to night.

Skylar surprised Tessa by pulling a harmonica from his

front pocket. After licking the mouthpiece, he began playing his approximation of a blues riff. Skylar was undoubtedly, unequivocally tone-deaf. And the most adorable part was that he had no idea. He was working so hard to make it sound good, but everything that emerged from the harmonica sounded like a duck being strangled. It took all of Tessa's willpower not to plug her ears and howl.

When Skylar finally finished, he was out of breath. "Pretty good, right?"

Unable to restrain herself any longer, Tessa burst out laughing. Skylar frowned and stuffed the harmonica back into his pants. She'd clearly hurt his feelings.

"Oh, no. I'm really sorry," Tessa said. "Obviously you haven't been doing it a long time."

"Just for three years."

Tessa felt her face drop. She was digging this hole even deeper. Thankfully, Skylar offered her a sweet, forgiving smile. "You should have heard me back then," he said. "My mom and dad started wearing earmuffs. In the summer."

They broke out in laughter, the tension released.

A breeze swept through the cracks in the windows. The soiled curtains began to bellow in a dance of fabric, only adding to the feeling that the room was haunted.

"Can you hear them?" Tessa asked.

"Hear who?"

"The ghosts of newlyweds past," she replied.

Skylar smiled, playing along. "What are they saying to each other?"

"The groom is saying…" Tessa's voice sank several octaves as she mimicked a man's voice. *"For God's sake, honey. You've been in the bathroom for two hours. You're my wife now, it's time to come to bed."*

"And the bride?" Skylar asked. "What's she saying?"

"The bride is saying…" This time, Tessa raised her voice to a high pitch. *"But you haven't kissed me once all day."*

The moment the words came out, she regretted them. Too forward, too thirsty.

Skylar turned and looked into Tessa's eyes. He seemed tentative, maybe even a little nervous. He touched her lower lip with the tip of his finger, tracing the curve of her mouth until he made a circle. Then he leaned in and pressed his lips to hers.

Tessa felt fireflies—racing and fluttering through her chest, making her feel as light as tissue paper, like she could just float up, through the roof of this old hotel, into the sky, past the seagulls, and into the clouds.

It wasn't just a kiss. It was epic.

Skylar parked in front of Tessa's house and cut the engine. "Want me to come in and meet your parents?" he asked. "Just so they know I'm not an a-hole jock?"

"Actually, they're not my parents."

"Oh?"

"They're just genetic strangers I live with."

"Genetic strangers?"

"I'm not related to either one of them. They're not my biological parents."

"Sounds like an...interesting story?" Skylar observed, fishing for a bit more.

"For another time," Tessa said.

Skylar took the hint and backed off. "So when can I see you again?"

"When are you back in Margate?"

"End of June. Right after I graduate."

"You'll be here for the whole summer? With your grandfather?"

"Yup. Until I leave for Brown."

Tessa nearly choked. *"Brown?* Hold up. Are you telling me I just kissed an Ivy League bro?"

"Is your street cred ruined?"

"Not unless you also work as a lifeguard?"

"Washington Avenue Beach."

"Gah! No way!" She groaned loudly for comedic effect, but Skylar quieted her with a long kiss. When he finally pulled away, Tessa had to make a conscious effort to remove the smile glued to her face.

"Good night," she said. "Thanks for dinner."

She walked to her front door, but Skylar stayed put. How

sweet. He was waiting to make sure she got inside okay. Tessa placed her key in the lock and swung around to wave goodbye to him. He nodded and pulled out. She watched his red taillights advance down the street, shrinking in size, until all she could hear was the distant rumble of his jeep's engine.

And then he was gone.

Inside now, Tessa closed the door and locked it. The foyer was dark. It was past eleven, and Vickie and Mel were probably asleep upstairs.

Alone for the first time in hours, Tessa was overcome with emotion. She couldn't explain why, but tears came to her eyes. At first, she thought they might be tears of happiness. But then she realized they were tears of *fear*. Deep down, Tessa sensed she was experiencing the first rush of love. And that didn't just scare her—it scared the living daylights out of her. Because for Tessa, love meant one thing only: pain. As a child, she'd suffered enough pain to last a lifetime. And it was never voluntary pain. It was always others who were responsible for her suffering. Manipulative foster moms, cruel foster dads, bullying foster siblings. Not to mention the original sin: the disappearance of her real mom and dad. But her feelings for Skylar were a different story. If things got serious with him and he broke her heart, Tessa would have no one to blame but herself.

She went upstairs to her bedroom, peeled off her jeans, and slipped into bed. Her lips were tingling, and they felt tender from all the kissing. She lifted her forearm to her nose, hoping for the faintest hint of Skylar's aroma on her skin.

A lot had transpired that night, and Tessa decided to spend the next hour replaying it from start to finish. At some point, her eyes closed, and sleep came. But there was no need to dream, because nothing could surpass the night she'd just had.

twenty
days
after

FOR TESSA'S FIRST DINNER HOME, VICKIE HAD OUTDONE HER-self. She ordered pizza from JoJo's, Tessa's favorite, and baked a cake from scratch, devil's food with vanilla frosting, also Tessa's favorite. Afterward came the gifts. New clothes, new sneakers, even a new iPhone. That was the problem with Vickie. She always overdid it. She never knew when to hit the brakes.

Mel was mostly silent. He had a big appetite, and any excuse to stray from his latest diet was a godsend. So long as they were celebrating, why couldn't he nick an extra slice of pizza and chocolate cake?

After gifts, Tessa excused herself from the table, claiming she felt exhausted and needed to lie down in her room. But the truth was, she felt an intense wave of sadness churning inside and knew the only way to alleviate it would be to cry. So she spent the next hour beneath her covers, sobbing until her stomach muscles went sore.

Afterward, Tessa glanced at the ceiling. By the middle of the summer, she'd removed her art photos and replaced them with black-and-whites she'd taken of Skylar. Her gaze swam over the joyous, frozen moments. Skylar's eyes, his tussled hair, his lazy smile, those fluffy, oh-so-kissable lips. Images and sensations from the summer tumbled over one another inside Tessa's mind, like a snowball rolling down a mountain, gaining mass and bulk, unleashing a ferocious, unstoppable avalanche of longing. Through the power of memory, Skylar was now so close that Tessa felt compelled to say something to him out loud.

"Skylar? Are you here...?"

She sat in silence for a few moments, then tried again. "Please, Skylar. If you're here, give me a sign...."

Tessa waited, hoping that one of her posters would fall to the floor or a windowpane would spontaneously splinter like they did in horror movies. She would accept anything as a sign. Even if her door flew open on its own or it started hailing golf balls outside.

But her posters held still, her windows didn't shatter, and not a single hailstone fell from the night sky.

twenty-
nine
days
after

ON THE SUNDAY BEFORE TESSA RETURNED TO SCHOOL, MEL suggested they go play some miniature golf. Since Vickie had volunteered for an extra shift at work, it would be just the two of them. "Come on," Mel said. "It'll cheer you up."

Tessa didn't have the energy to say no.

Chuck's Mini Golf was on the bay side of the island, and since the summer was officially over, there were only a few families playing the course that cloudy afternoon.

Mel paid the front-desk clerk in cash. He and Tessa chose two putters and two different-colored balls, then set out to play the course. There were eighteen holes in all, a mismatch of nautical themes, lighthouses, and windmills. Tessa didn't even register she was playing golf until the eighth green, when she struck her ball and it miraculously banked around a cork-screw of artificial turf and dropped into the hole.

"Hole in one!" Mel yelled, raising his hand for a high five. Tessa tapped his palm weakly and bent over to retrieve her ball.

As they walked to the next hole, Mel surprised Tessa with a little piece of history. "You know," he said, "this is where I took your mom on our first date."

Mel rarely talked about Tessa's biological mom. And yet, there were times when she sensed a deep heartache inside him, struggling to find its voice. Ironically, that was what made Mel the ideal father figure for Tessa. She didn't like to talk about her feelings, either.

"I never knew that," Tessa said.

"She had an amazing putting stroke. Beat me by *twelve* shots. Afterward, we walked over to the Greenhouse and had a couple of beers. We got pretty buzzed, and then...she laid one on me."

"You mean, Mom kissed you first?"

He nodded. "Sure took the pressure off. The second she pulled away, I looked into her eyes and I was a goner. I mean, head over heels."

It was hard to imagine Mel as a lovestruck guy, swooning after a first kiss.

Mel's smile sank, replaced by a wistful sadness. "When she ditched out on me, I didn't know what to do. I was like a chicken without a head. I kept expecting her to come back, hoping everything would return to normal, but it never did. And I was one hundred percent certain I'd never love another woman again. But then..." His smile returned. "I met Vickie."

Now Tessa understood what this outing was *really* about. It wasn't some lovely father-daughter bonding thing. It was a pep talk. Mel was trying to explain that—even though Tessa had loved Skylar—she'd find someone else; she'd love again.

It was such a Mel thing to say. His heart, as always, was in the right place. But his timing couldn't have been worse. It had barely been a month since she'd lost Skylar, and Mel was already telling her there were more fish in the sea?

Tessa wanted to feel upset but couldn't generate the strength to scold him. Instead, all she could manage was "I'm tired, Mel, can we go home?"

Tessa dropped her club where she was standing, turned, and headed off to the parking lot.

thirty
days
after

"TESSA!" VICKIE SCREAMED. "SHANNON'S OUT FRONT, SHE'S honking!"

Tessa glanced at her clock. Shit! It was 7:25. If she didn't hustle, she'd be late for her first day back at school. Tessa grabbed her new iPhone and scooped her backpack off the floor. As she rushed out of her room, Vickie called after her. "Wait a sec—aren't you forgetting something?"

"I'm not giving you a kiss goodbye, Vickie."

Vickie unhooked Tessa's Minolta from the doorknob and held it out for her. "Your camera."

"Thanks. But I didn't forget it," Tessa said.

"What do you mean? You take your camera everywhere."

Tessa ignored Vickie's question, charged down the stairs, and pushed through the front door. Across the lawn, she spotted Shannon parked at the curb, sitting inside her brand-new car....

A white Hyundai?

When Tessa climbed in, she could see embarrassment on Shannon's face. Shannon never hid her feelings. If she was happy, you knew it. And if she wasn't, you damn well knew that, too.

Shannon's eyes narrowed with simmering anger. "One A...three Cs," she explained. "*Three* Cs and I'm stuck with this...this...!" She trailed off, unable to muster the right insult for her new car.

"Damn," Tessa said. "Your dad is—"

"An emotionally detached asshole?"

"I was gonna say sensible."

"I'm gonna tint the windows so no one knows it's me inside."

"Enough whining," Tessa said. "Take me to jail."

Shannon pushed the gear into *Drive* and pulled out, but then she abruptly jammed down on the brakes. "Hold up. Where's your camera?"

"Never mind," Tessa said.

Shannon pushed the gear back into *Park*. "It's fine. Go get it—I'll wait."

"Shannon? It's my first day back, I don't want to be late."

Shannon chose not to press the matter, though her expression revealed an ember of concern. She'd once observed that Tessa without her camera was like Van Gogh without his paintbrush.

Shannon turned up the music and pulled out of Exeter Court. When she reached the stop sign at the end of the street, she surprised Tessa by turning left onto Douglas Avenue. That was strange. Shannon had picked Tessa up a zillion times using her mom's car and had *never* turned left here. She *always* turned right.

Unless... yes, that was it.... Shannon was deliberately avoiding Skylar's grandfather's house. She was worried that seeing it might set Tessa off, so she changed her usual route, like a GPS redirecting a driver to avoid a traffic jam.

There were more detours to come. Shannon avoided North Clermont Avenue because that was where the accident had taken place. Then she did some serious zigzagging to avoid driving past the Little Art Theater. Tessa considered scolding her friend for all the driving gymnastics but realized it came from a place of concern, so chose to remain silent.

"Did you call the phone company?" Shannon asked.

Tessa nodded.

"So what did they say?"

"They said Skylar probably texted the photo before the accident happened—and it was sitting on the server until the phone was turned on."

"Uh, hello. That's what I said."

"That still doesn't explain how my phone turned on, even though it was totally trashed. Explain that."

"I can't," Shannon replied. "But I'm pretty sure it wasn't Skylar who turned it on."

Tessa deflated. Of course Skylar hadn't turned her phone on from the afterworld. Skylar was dead. His body had been buried weeks ago. And his life—and everything he'd shared with Tessa—was now just a memory.

At that moment, the song on Shannon's Spotify mix ended...and another song began. It only took a moment for Tessa to recognize the opening guitar licks of the Roxy Music song "More Than This." Sadness swelled inside her.

Frantic, Shannon fumbled for her phone. "Shit!" She quickly pressed the arrow button on the screen and advanced to the next song. But the damage had been done.

"Sorry," Shannon said. "You put it on my mix."

"It's okay," Tessa said.

But it wasn't okay. Hearing the song brought the whole summer back. Tessa's head sank, a curtain of hair draping over her face. With her eyes now hidden, the tears came easily.

Seeing her friend's distress, Shannon swerved to the side of the road and parked. She wrapped Tessa in her arms. "It's gonna be okay," she insisted. "We'll get through this. I swear."

Tessa choked back tears. "I never got to say goodbye."

"I know."

"I don't even remember the last thing I said to him....What if it was something bitchy?"

"Come on—"

"I'm serious. We were fighting that last week, remember?"

"Tess, you need to forget what you *don't* remember and focus on what you *do*. You guys had, like, *the* epic summer.

You'll never forget it. Hell, I won't forget it and I was just a jealous bystander."

Tessa managed a smile. She lifted her chin off Shannon's shoulder, leaving behind a stain of tears on her friend's shirt. "I just wish I could have one more day with him...one more hour."

"I'm sure he feels the same way," Shannon assured her. "Wherever he is."

Just then, Tessa caught her reflection in the rearview mirror and moaned. "Great. My first day back and I look like a total disaster."

"Chill. Mama's gonna glow you up."

Shannon dug through her overstuffed purse and located some concealer and blush. She quickly got to work buffing away Tessa's sadness.

"Tess, I don't want to freak you out, but I think you should be prepared for today."

"Prepared for what?"

"It's your first day back at school. And everyone knows about the accident—that you 'died' and came back. It was in the newspaper."

"Oh, Jesus."

"Exactly. You've risen from the dead. We're talking Stormborn, Mother of Dragons. All I'm saying is—be ready."

Be ready.

Truer words had never been spoken.

Everyone in school knew about the accident.

Every student, every teacher, even the janitors knew. And because everyone knew, everyone was staring at Tessa, the girl whose heart had stopped beating for two minutes. And these were not subtle glances. They were long, drawn-out, gaping looks. The kind of looks that Tessa could feel from behind, like waves of heat radiating onto her back. Tessa now understood why movie stars were often caught attacking paparazzi, snatching their cameras and smashing them to the pavement. Life was not meant to be lived under a microscope. Sooner or later, everyone snapped.

Tessa slammed her locker shut. Gerald, her one and only fanboy, was standing beside her. He was trembling, having difficulty forming a word. "H-h-hey, T-Tessa," he stammered.

Tessa did not want to talk to Gerald, but suspected he was here to offer his condolences, and that was more than she could say for the rest of her classmates.

"I j-just wanted to, you know—"

"Offer your condolences?" Tessa said.

"Uh-huh."

"Thanks, Gerald," Tessa said, patting his shoulder. "I gotta go."

She left Gerald standing at her locker. He looked sad, but lucky for him, he didn't know what real sadness was.

Tessa was in the school cafeteria, poking at a clump of under-cooked french fries.

"Welcome back, Tessa."

When she looked up, she saw Mr. Duffy sitting across the table from her, a paisley tie hanging between the lapels of his corduroy jacket. His expression was laced with genuine concern. "I heard what happened. I'm terribly sorry for your loss."

What else could Tessa say but "thank you."

"At the risk of sounding insensitive," he said, "use it."

"Use what?"

"The pain. The emptiness. Everything you're feeling. Channel it through your camera. Some of the greatest works of art were produced by intense grief."

Her life was totally wrecked, and Mr. Duffy was now trying to convince her that it was a good thing?

"And don't forget—the RISD early-application deadline is in November. It would be a shame if you let the opportunity slip away."

College applications? Was he serious? She couldn't take a single breath without her insides wanting to explode into a fireball of rage and sadness. And this hippie with the bushy mustache was trying to talk about her future?

The bell rang. Tessa grabbed her bag, rose to her feet, and walked away.

She didn't say goodbye to Mr. Duffy.

thirty-three days after

TESSA HAD SPENT COUNTLESS HOURS WORKING IN HER ATTIC darkroom. But it only took her fifteen minutes to pack it up. Her enlarger fit into one box. Her chemicals and assorted paraphernalia fit into another. She *did* think twice about trashing her negatives. After all, there were no backups, digital or otherwise. If Tessa trashed her negatives, there'd be no turning back. Everything she had captured over the past few years would be lost forever.

She knew she was being rash and childish, but she didn't care. If the world was going to deny her Skylar, then she was going to deny the world her one and only talent. She'd no longer look through her viewfinder, because all she'd see was emptiness and absence, a rectangle that was missing Skylar.

One by one, Tessa carried the boxes down the stairs, out the back door, and across the side lawn. At the curb, she stacked them like giant Lego blocks, right next to the garbage cans. There would be no burial and no eulogy for her darkroom. Instead, while she slept, a stranger from the sanitation department would hurl its contents into the back of their truck, erasing this chapter of Tessa's life forever.

"You know, we spent a heckuva lot of money on that stuff."

Tessa turned. Mel was standing behind her. He was dressed in a faded bathrobe, his hair askew. Vickie must have woken him from a nap and ordered him to go talk to her.

"Send me the bill," Tessa replied. "I'll pay you back."

"So that's it? You're just . . . giving up your photography?"

"Looks like it."

Tessa moved to leave, but Mel blocked her path. "You know, this is the kind of crap your mom used to pull. She'd become obsessed with things. Baking. Yoga. Pottery—"

"Men?"

Mel's face tightened. "Yes. Men too. Then one day, she'd lose interest and move on to the next. That's why she could never get any traction in life. That's why she could never be a real mother to you."

"Lecture over?" Tessa asked, her voice dripping with sarcasm.

Mel just stood there, flummoxed and silent. She knew that fathering didn't come naturally to him, but that never stopped him from trying.

As Tessa headed back to the house, Mel called out: "Do you think Skylar would have wanted this?"

"I don't know, Mel. Why don't you ask him?"

eighty-
nine
days
before

THE MORNING AFTER THEIR FIRST KISS, TESSA WOKE UP WORRY-
ing the date was just a dream. Nights like that didn't happen
in real life. It was too easy to be with Skylar. It was like they'd
known each other forever. Did he feel the same way about her,
or was she just imagining the intensity of their connection?

Tessa reached for her phone on the nightstand. There were
seventeen missed calls from Shannon. Obviously, Tessa's bestie was desperate to know what had gone down last night. Also
on her phone was a short text from Skylar. A text so sweet, it
immediately extinguished Tessa's paranoia about what she'd
experienced with him.

SKYLAR: Thanks for last night. Great food, awesome convo,
amazing kisser.

Over the next several weeks, they exchanged texts and emails and FaceTimed often. They asked each other lots of questions and told each other about the things they loved and hated. It turned out they shared similar taste in music—'80s New Wave, '90s trip-hop, Frank Ocean, Travis Scott. But they completely disagreed on *The Handmaid's Tale*. Tessa loved it. Skylar felt it was totally overrated and only appealed to angry women. Skylar's final death-row meal would be chicken Parmesan and cheesecake. Tessa's would be pizza and devil's food cake.

Skylar gave Tessa a video tour of his bedroom. His walls were covered with posters of exotic beaches in New Zealand and Fiji. He said he wasn't sure what his future held but knew he wanted to put all his languages to use. After college, he intended to travel the world, read books, meet new people, and row in more rivers than he could count.

When Skylar asked Tessa about her future plans, she remained elusive. How could she tell an Ivy League boy she had no real interest in college? Vickie and Mel had already warned her they didn't have the means to pay for her tuition. The likeliest scenario for Tessa was a two-year degree from a community college. After that, she'd get a job at one of the local casinos, working to pay off the loans she'd taken out for her worthless diploma.

Because Skylar rose before dawn to train and row, there was often a text waiting for Tessa when she woke in the morning. Usually, it was something playful—a joke or a silly GIF. But as their connection deepened, their texts grew sexier and more intimate.

SKYLAR: Tell me a secret.

TESSA: ???

SKYLAR: Tell me something you've never told anyone else in the world.

SKYLAR: Hello? Did I scare you away?

TESSA: Thinking...

TESSA: Ok. When I was six, I was in a store with my mom and I wanted her to buy me a pack of stickers and she said no. So I stole them.

SKYLAR: Su-weet!

TESSA: But then I felt really guilty for stealing them, so I wrote a letter to God and asked him to forgive me and I buried it in the backyard.

SKYLAR: We need to go and dig that letter up.

TESSA: I believe God already did that. ☺ Okay, your turn. Tell me a secret.

SKYLAR: I have a man-crush on Billy Joel.

TESSA: Lol! That's not a real secret!

SKYLAR: Ok, fine....This is something that no one else knows. And I'm telling you in total confidence. I can trust you, right?

TESSA: I'm insulted you'd even ask.

SKYLAR: Here goes...

TESSA: Sky?

TESSA: Helloooooooooooo?

TESSA: Oh come on!

SKYLAR: I think about you.

SKYLAR: A lot.

SKYLAR: Are you still there?

TESSA: How much is "a lot"?

SKYLAR: Um, basically EVERY WAKING MOMENT.

TESSA: Come kiss me.

SKYLAR: Give me an hour.

Was he really going to drive down to kiss her? Tessa knew that Skylar had a final exam that day, but he'd already been accepted to Brown, and no test outcome could undo that.

Sure enough, a little over sixty minutes later, Skylar's jeep pulled up outside of Tessa's house. His rowing shell was affixed to his roof, covered in white canvas. She noticed his engine radiating waves of heat from beneath the hood. Eager boy, he must have driven like a speed demon.

Skylar stepped out of his jeep. Tessa had gotten so used to seeing him on her iPhone screen, she'd forgotten how tall he was. He'd obviously come straight from his morning row and was still wearing his training tights, which made her giggle. His hair was a wonderful, floppy mess.

Heartbeat thudding, Tessa greeted him on the lawn with a sheepish smile. "I can't believe you came."

Without answering, Skylar kissed her. God, it was like their lips had been molded in a factory so that they fit together perfectly. For a fleeting moment, Tessa considered pulling Skylar upstairs into her bedroom. But she held herself in check. There would be plenty of time for hooking up during the summer.

Skylar finally stepped back, green eyes luminous in the

morning sun. "Sorry. Gotta go—I have an exam. See you in a few weeks?"

Tessa nodded, still savoring the kiss.

"Oh," Skylar said. "Almost forgot." He reached through his jeep's open window and handed Tessa a thin, brown paper bag. Surprised, she pulled out what was inside. It was a pack of stickers.

"Sorry. All they had was Pokémon."

Tessa beamed with appreciation. "Pokémon's the shit."

"True dat."

Skylar climbed back into his jeep, fired up the engine, and tore out.

It took all of Tessa's effort not to faint on her lawn.

seventy-
five
days
before

IF EVER THERE WAS A PERFECT DAY TO CUT SCHOOL, THIS WAS IT.
For starters, it was the final week of classes, and everyone—
including Tessa's teachers—was mentally checked out. More
important, though, was the photography exhibit. Weeks
earlier, Tessa had read that the Philadelphia Museum of Art
would be presenting a program called *The City of Light and Its
Shadows*. The exhibit featured the work of Brassaï, a French
photographer who'd documented the nighttime streets of
Paris between World War I and World War II. Brassaï's photos combined two of Tessa's greatest obsessions: high-contrast
black-and-white photography and Paris of the past.

Tessa had only seen Brassaï's work on the internet, mostly
as low-res JPEGs. But it was incredibly challenging to learn
about his technique when she was looking at photos of photos.

In person, she could study Brassaï's frame selection and his use of natural light. She could also examine his printing technique, which produced a richness and depth that Tessa found astonishingly beautiful.

Unfortunately, there were two problems in Tessa's way. Problem one? The exhibition was ending that day, and Tessa had no way of getting up to Philadelphia. Unless she could persuade Shannon to drive her, which was problem two. Shannon and museums were like peanut butter and ham—they didn't mesh. If Tessa asked Shannon to cut school for something cultural, it would be a quick *hell no*. Tessa needed to lure her best friend with something more enticing.

"Let's cut school, drive up to Philly, and go shopping," Tessa blurted out as she and Shannon walked through the schoolyard.

Shannon appeared suspicious. She knew that Tessa had little or no interest in fashion or clothes. Not to mention, Tessa didn't come from a rich family like Shannon did. If Tessa ever had any money in her pocket, she spent it on darkroom supplies.

"Shopping?" Shannon said. "You can't be serious."

Tessa had already prepared an answer, and it wasn't a lie. "Skylar's coming back to Margate next week. He asked me to have dinner with him and his grandfather, and I want to wear something cute."

Shannon raised an eyebrow. "Hold up. It's his first night back in Margate and he's bringing along a chaperone?"

"He's super close with his grandfather and wants me to meet him. I think it's cute."

As they continued walking, Shannon looked up to the sky to scrutinize the weather, seemingly trying to determine if the drive would be worth it. A sunny day made boutique hopping so much easier. Finally, Shannon stopped in her tracks. "Fine. I'll take you up to Philly on one condition."

"Anything."

"You have to let me pick out your dress," Shannon said.

Leave it to Shannon to ask for the one thing Tessa feared most. Shannon's taste in clothes was, to put it mildly, slutty. She was constantly pressuring Tessa to flash more skin, more cleavage, and more thigh. If Shannon had her way, Tessa would show up at Skylar's grandfather's house dressed in a see-through teddy. On the other hand, if that was the price Tessa had to pay to see Brassaï's work, so be it.

"It's got to be a casual dress," Tessa warned. "It's just dinner with Gramps, not a weekend in Vegas. You feel me?"

"Yeah," Shannon said. "I feel you."

Ten minutes later, they were heading north on the Atlantic City Expressway. Barring traffic, they'd arrive in Philadelphia by ten. Once there, Tessa would happily indulge Shannon's every shopping whim. Only after lunch, with Shannon in a state of retail therapy bliss, would Tessa mention the museum.

Just then, Tessa's cell phone vibrated.

"Boat boy wants to FaceTime," Shannon said, pointing to the phone on Tessa's lap. Tessa pressed *Accept*. The screen came to life, and Skylar appeared dressed in a cap and gown, clutching a copy of his diploma. "Holla!" he shouted.

He looked undeniably cute, his curls hanging out from beneath the blue satin cap that sat askew on his head.

"Congratulations!" Tessa said. "How'd your speech go?"

"Pretty well, I think. I was *way* more nervous than I expected."

Shannon interrupted. "Don't tell me he was valedictorian?"

"No, just class president," Tessa replied.

"Yawn," Shannon said.

"Is that Shannon?" Skylar asked from the other side of the phone.

"It is!" Shannon screamed. "Hi, Skylar!"

Tessa swung her phone around and pointed it at Shannon, who flashed a smile. The prior month, Tessa had introduced Shannon and Skylar via FaceTime, and thank God they'd taken a liking to each other. "I hear you're finally getting your ass back to the shore. You ready to party?"

"That's the plan," Skylar said. "Where you guys headed?"

Tessa jumped back in. "Philly. There's this great photo exhibition at—" Tessa stopped herself. Dammit. She'd let it slip.

"Photo exhibition?" Shannon's face slackened as she realized she'd been played by her best friend. "Wait. You bait and switched me?"

Tessa turned back to the screen. "Sky? Can I call you later? I gotta do some damage control here."

"Copy that. Have fun, kids. Au revoir," he said, and then the screen went blank.

At this point, Tessa felt the best defense was a good offense. "Come on, Shan. We both know you could use a little more culture."

"I get plenty of culture. I read Goop religiously."

"Trust me, you're gonna love Brassaï."

"*Brassaï?* It sounds like a venereal disease."

"He was a genius," Tessa said. "And his work is very accessible."

Without answering, Shannon hit the blinker and veered off at the nearest exit.

"Oh, come on," Tessa said, "you're not turning around!"

"Can't a girl pee?"

Shannon pulled into a service station and disappeared around back. While waiting, Tessa stepped out of the car to get some fresh air. That was when she noticed an old, rusted bridge hanging over a narrow river about fifty yards away. Its curved arches were suspended to steel girders with gigantic rivets, all of them the color of burnt orange. Something about this crumbling, industrial-size monstrosity was utterly compelling to Tessa.

As if under a spell, Tessa reached into the back seat of Shannon's car and scooped up her camera. She walked from the service station lot, climbed over a concrete embankment, and arrived at one end of the bridge, which was cordoned off with a chain-link fence. There were several graffiti-riddled DO NOT TRESPASS signs, but Tessa ignored them and scaled the fence anyway. She began to wander across the old bridge, taking photos of whatever struck her as interesting.

There was something poetic about decayed objects. They weren't ugly; they simply expressed a different kind of beauty: a hidden beauty, the kind only accessible to one's imagination. It was like seeing an old movie star, knowing full well what they once looked like when they were young and glamorous.

Tessa realized she could get more interesting photos of the bridge from beneath it. She climbed back over the fence and walked down the dirt hill, making her way to the water's edge. She raised her camera and looked through her viewfinder but wasn't satisfied. The angle from here wasn't dynamic enough. The best spot would be in the middle of the river. She needed to get into the water.

Tessa sat on the dirt and pulled off her shoes, then her socks, which she tucked into little balls and stuffed into her sneakers. She peeled off her jeans and T-shirt and piled them on top of her sneakers so they wouldn't touch the ground. Now dressed only in a bra and a pair of boy shorts, Tessa rose to her feet and faced the river.

"Yo! What the heck are you doing?" Shannon yelled as she struggled down the dirt incline.

"Just taking some photos," Tessa said.

"With your clothes off?"

"I can get a much better angle in there," Tessa said, pointing to the river that flowed beneath the bridge.

"In the river? There's, like, toxic sludge in there."

"I'll only be in the water for a minute."

Shannon crossed her arms. "Twenty years from now, when your doctor tells you the bump in your tummy is not a baby but a tumor, just remember I was against this."

"Sure you don't want to join me?"

"Is it heated?"

Tessa inhaled deeply, steeling herself, then took her first tentative step into the water. The searing cold around her foot was far worse than she expected, and she quickly stepped back to the muddy shoreline.

"That went well," Shannon said. "Can we go now?"

"No. I can do this."

Tessa stepped back in, one foot followed by the other. The river's muddy floor felt squishy beneath her soles. She stood in place for a few moments, allowing her feet to acclimate to the water's icy coldness. Everything inside her body was telling her to turn back, but dammit, she wanted that photo, so she willed herself forward.

Suddenly, the river's bottom dropped out from beneath her. Panicked, Tessa lifted her camera over her head and began kicking her legs to keep herself afloat.

Shannon shouted from the shore. "You okay?"

"It's deeper than I thought!"

"Want me to call Skylar and have him come rescue you?"

Thankfully, the current was gentle. Using only a single hand, Tessa paddled out to the middle of the river. Wading beneath the bridge, she looked through her viewfinder and knew she'd made the right choice. The light, the shadows, the river's shimmering reflections on the underside of the bridge. It was perfect. She took as many photos as she could before she ran out of film.

Tessa swam back to shore. She found Shannon sitting on the dirt next to her clothes. She was on her phone, trading texts with someone. There was a feverish smile on her face, as if she'd just won a raffle.

"What is it?" Tessa asked.

Shannon looked up and waved her phone. "Judd just asked me out."

For her sweet sixteen, Shannon's dad had given her an American Express Gold Card, and she was not shy about using it. After three hours in Philadelphia, Shannon had bought herself bagfuls of makeup and hair product, an entire summer wardrobe, and a bikini so skimpy, it would make a Kardashian blush.

Tessa didn't really like anything she saw, but Shannon persuaded her to buy a ruffled summer dress. Even though it was on sale, it still wiped out most of Tessa's savings. Thankfully, she'd be starting her summer job the following week.

In the afternoon, the girls had a long lunch at Shannon's

favorite café in Rittenhouse Square. Tessa wanted to order a cheeseburger and fries but then remembered that Skylar would be coming next week. She'd seen what he looked like with his shirt off. Part boy, part demigod. She chose a salad instead.

By the time they arrived at the museum, it was nearly four, which meant Tessa would have only an hour to tour the exhibit.

Brassaï's work was even more powerful in person. There was a reason why his nickname was "the Eye of Paris." It wasn't just the quality of his photos that impressed Tessa but his attention to detail. His street scenes were foggy and gray, the pavements shiny and slick from a recent storm. And there were often shafts of light cutting through his frames to create visual excitement and depth of field.

Even Shannon loved the exhibit, especially Brassaï's photos of Parisian nightlife. The men and women were dressed to the nines, drinking champagne, smoking cigarettes from holders, and enjoying the gaiety of Paris in the 1930s and '40s.

On the drive home, they were both exhausted and barely spoke. When Shannon dropped Tessa off, they hugged good-bye, holding each other a little bit longer than usual. With her best friend in her arms, Tessa somehow sensed this would be a day she'd never forget.

Before Shannon drove away, she lowered her window and called out to Tessa: "You know you're my bestie, right?"

"Forever and eva," Tessa said back.

sixty-
five
days
before

Jackpot gifts was one of three souvenir shops owned by Harold Goldman. Back in the '80s and '90s, enough tourists visited Atlantic City that Harold was able to keep his stores on the Boardwalk open throughout the year. But after neighboring states introduced their own forms of gambling, Harold's foot traffic slowed, as did his sales. Eventually, he had no choice but to switch to a seasonal model. His stores were now open during the summer months only, from Memorial Day to Labor Day.

It was the end of June, and it was Tessa's second summer working at Jackpot. Enjoying a temporary lull, she wandered to the front of the store and stood beneath an enormous air-conditioning vent, cooling herself while watching the crowds outside on the Boardwalk. She saw tourists of all shapes and sizes passing in both directions, some of them being pushed in canopied rolling chairs. In the distance, she could see the ocean surf and hear the joyful shrieks of children playing on the beach.

"You look different this summer," Harold said.

Tessa turned and saw the owner, Harold, standing at the register. He had entered through the back door and was counting out some cash. Harold was on the shorter side of five seven, with a deep tan and a thick head of salt-and-pepper hair. He was wearing lime-green shorts, a collared pink shirt, and brown leather loafers. The clash of colors in his daily outfits always brought a grin to Tessa's face.

"Different how?" Tessa asked.

"Happier?"

Tessa glowered. "Define happiness."

"When I was your age, happiness meant finding a pretty girl to kiss. At my age now—I'm fifty-nine, by the way—happiness means hitting a trifecta."

Tessa did not know what a trifecta was, but she guessed it had something to do with gambling, which was Harold's not-so-secret hobby.

"Did you meet a nice boy?" Harold asked.

Tessa held back a smile.

"Good for you," he said. "A shoebee?"

Shoebee. It was a term that only locals knew. It was slang for out-of-towners, people who wore shoes on the beach.

"He lives up north, but he's not a shoebee. He spends his

summers down here. He's actually coming down tomorrow night. I'm seeing him for the first time in a while. He asked me to have dinner with him and his grandfather."

"Are you nervous?" Harold asked, but before Tessa could reply, he cut in: "Don't be. Believe me, he's even more nervous than you are."

"How do you know?" Tessa asked.

"Because I was a teenage boy once, too," he said, slamming the register drawer shut. "Just make sure you bring a gift tomorrow night."

"A gift?"

"Of course. You've got to make a good impression, right? Bring dessert. That's what I'd bring. Better yet, bake a cake. It'll have the personal touch."

With that, Harold exited the store, no doubt en route to one of the city's blackjack tables.

sixty-
four
days
before

Skylar's first text of the night came at 6:52 pm.

SKYLAR: Are you on your way?

Tessa did not respond.

Ten minutes later, her phone rang. She let it go to voice mail. When she played the message back, she heard Skylar's voice. *"Hey, it's Skylar. Uh . . . I texted you. . . . Is everything okay? Where are you? Call me back."*

She did not call him back.

Tessa was inside Vickie's SUV, parked on North Clermont Avenue. She was barely a block away from Skylar's grandfather's house, a hundred yards at most. But she'd been sitting there for a half hour, frozen, immobile.

The day hadn't started out like this.

It had begun with Tessa attempting, and failing, to make

a chocolate cake. Harold had been right: Dessert was a great idea. Unfortunately, Tessa had about as much skill in the kitchen as she did at nuclear physics. Vickie offered to help, but genius that Tessa was, she insisted on doing it herself. How hard could it be to bake a cake?

The instant Tessa pulled the pan out of the oven, she knew something was terribly wrong. The cake didn't even look like cake; it looked like a lopsided blob of chocolate. Tessa figured she could cover her mistake with the icing but didn't realize you couldn't put icing on warm cake. Immediately after spreading the icing across the top, it began melting, oozing down the sides of the cake like molten lava. Tessa tried putting the cake into the refrigerator, hoping to cool it down. But twenty minutes later, the cake still looked like an abomination, only colder. Tessa eventually surrendered. She scraped the entire mess into the garbage, deciding she'd pick something up on the way over to Skylar's.

Tessa showered, fixed her hair, then pulled on the dress she had bought with Shannon in Philly. Why oh why did clothes always look so much better when you wore them in the store? Were the rumors true that clothing stores hung special mirrors in their dressing rooms that made you look skinnier? Oh hell, Tessa didn't have time for this. Skylar had asked her to be there at six thirty and it was already six fifteen.

Tessa drove to Dottie's Pastry Shop, a hole-in-the-wall bakery on Ventnor Avenue. It was near closing time, and Tessa panicked when she saw all the display cases empty. Thankfully,

Dottie was able to cobble together a selection of cookies from the back. She placed them in a square box, which she wrapped tightly in baker's string.

As Tessa got closer to Skylar's house, an icy sweat began to form on her neck. She cranked up the air conditioner. But that made her shiver. Now she was cold and anxious. And maybe a little bit nauseous, too. She wondered if she was having a panic attack. She'd once read a list of the symptoms on the internet. She recalled that the best way to handle a panic attack was to stop what you were doing and breathe. So Tessa pulled the SUV to the side of the street, cut the engine, and began to breathe.

Inhale... exhale... inhale... exhale...

Outside the car, the sky began growing darker.

Inhale... exhale... inhale... exhale...

Through the windshield, Tessa saw the streetlights blink on simultaneously. One of them appeared to be broken. It was flickering like a strobe light.

Inhale... exhale... inhale... exhale...

When Tessa thought about it, what did she really know about Skylar? After all, they'd only spent a single night together. Granted, they'd traded quite a few texts and emails. But it was easy to be clever and witty when you had time to formulate your words.

Inhale... exhale... inhale... exhale...

How could Tessa know for sure that Skylar was the earnest, upbeat person he'd presented to her? And if Skylar *was* that person, what the hell did he want with Tessa? She was the opposite of upbeat. She had what Vickie called "an artist's temperament." Which was a nice way of saying that Tessa was depressed.

Tessa suddenly remembered something that one of her foster fathers told her. She had worked hard to blank out the man's name and face but would never forget something he'd said to her. *Maybe nobody wants you because you're not lovable.*

Not lovable.

They were so different, Skylar and her.

Skylar was lovable and knew it. You could see it in the way he held himself, the way he smiled, his confidence, the sparkle in his eyes. By all accounts, Skylar had been raised in a loving environment, with parents who were high school sweethearts. That did something to a kid. It bolstered them. Made them confident. Secure. The kind of kid who went to an Ivy League school and secretly looked down on people who didn't.

Sure, Tessa and Skylar might have some superficial things in common. But the differences in their pasts would inevitably get in the way. He'd get sick of her moods; she'd get sick of him smiling all the time. So why even bother? Why start a summer romance when the end was preordained? Wouldn't it be best for all parties if Tessa saved them the heartache now? Wouldn't she be doing him a favor? *Let Skylar go find another girl, a happy girl, with happy eyes like his.*

Tessa's phone *pinged.*

She looked down at her screen. It was a text from Skylar.

SKYLAR: ???????????

She did not reply.

thirty-four days after

"GO AWAY," TESSA CROAKED FROM HER BED. "I'M SLEEPING."

Her door opened anyway, flooding the room with light. Tessa squinted. She saw Vickie standing in her doorway, dressed in her casino dealer's uniform. She looked peeved. "Come on, Tess. It's past eight. I did a double shift and you were sleeping when I left.... Did you even go to school?"

Tessa yanked her blanket over her head. She heard Vickie release a frustrated sigh.

"You need to change your chest dressing. Not to mention get some food in your stomach."

"I'm not hungry."

"You haven't eaten a decent meal in days. That can't be healthy."

"I'll come down in a little while, I promise."

Satisfied, Vickie moved to shut the door. But before she could close it, Mel appeared behind her and poked his head into the room. "Hey, Tess?" he said. "I'm glad you changed your mind about the darkroom. It would have been a shame if you'd gotten rid of all that stuff."

Vickie pulled the door shut, returning the bedroom to darkness. It took Tessa a few moments for Mel's words to sink in. What did he mean, *changed her mind*? She hadn't changed her mind about her darkroom. What was he talking about?

Curious, Tessa climbed out of bed, crossed into the hallway, and pulled open the attic door. Halfway up the stairs, Tessa could already see that the safelights were on, casting an eerie red glow onto the slanted ceiling. When she finally crested the stairwell, she was stunned to discover that her darkroom had been completely reassembled. Every single object she'd packed up— every tray, every bottle, every tack on the corkboard—had been returned to where it had once been. Even the photos clipped to the clothesline had been put back in the exact order that she had originally hung them.

Tessa's first thought was that Mel must have done this. In an expression of fatherly concern, he had spent all night retrieving her equipment from the curb and returning it to the attic. But then she wondered how Mel could have known exactly where everything belonged, to the inch. And how did he manage to reassemble her enlarger? Mel could barely figure out how to use the toaster.

Which left Vickie.

But Tessa remembered Vickie telling her that she'd worked a double shift last night. Exactly when would she have done this?

Tessa became conscious of a low humming sound. Her eyes traced the room, and that was when she discovered her enlarger was actually on, its fan whirring methodically inside. Suddenly—FLASH!—the enlarger's lamp spontaneously fired off on its own. A chill of fear raced through Tessa's body. What the hell was happening here?

She moved closer to the enlarger and noticed a blank piece of photographic paper had been wedged into the baseboard easel. Curious, she reached up and removed the negative carrier but found it empty. This meant that the blank sheet in the baseboard would have no image at all. But there was only one way to be certain.

Tessa twisted the knob on her old kitchen timer and dropped the photo paper into the tray filled with developing solution....

She wasn't sure what she expected to see as she waited for the photo to develop. But the one thing she *didn't* expect to see was the color blue. Not just any blue. Electric blue, spreading like neon tendrils across the surface of the paper.

It made no sense. The chemicals she'd just mixed were strictly for black-and-white film. The presence of color on the photographic paper wasn't just a surprise—it was a scientific impossibility. Yet still, more colors bled across the surface of the paper, oranges and greens, forming misshapen blots, eventually joining to form a stack of letters....

O
R
RI
H
D
F
O

She tried to read the letters going up, then going down. But they did not form comprehensible words. More blots spread across the paper, forming more letters....

OU
RE
ERI
HE
AND
OF
OV

Tessa caught her breath when the final string of letters appeared, sandwiching around the others, forming the words:

YOU
ARE
ENTERING
THE

LAND
OF
LOVE

The words that welcomed guests to the Empyrean Hotel.

Ding!

Tessa was startled by the timer going off. She scrambled for a pair of tongs, lifted the dripping photo from the tray, and dropped it into the neighboring one with stop solution. She watched in shock as the photo continued developing, the letters growing darker and bleeding into one another. There was nothing she could do but watch the paper transform into a black rectangle. Until finally, the words were gone.

Tessa decided there were two possibilities to explain what had just happened:

1. Skylar was reaching out from the afterlife.

2. She was *imagining* Skylar was reaching out from the afterlife.

After considering her options, Tessa concluded there was only one way to confirm which explanation was correct. She needed to give Skylar another chance.

Tessa slipped a sheet of blank photo paper into the enlarger's baseboard. Then took a few steps back and said out loud: "Do it again, Sky."

She watched the enlarger, listening to its fan whirring. Nothing happened. She waited five, then ten minutes. Still nothing. With increasing anxiety, Tessa realized that possibility two was seeming more likely. She didn't want to be here anymore and felt the sudden urge to run out of her darkroom and never come back. Tessa reached beneath the enlarger to flip the *Off* switch when—FLASH!—it happened again.

Tessa quickly removed the paper and dropped it into the developing tray, submerging it beneath a pool of chemicals. Once again, a color photo came to life before her eyes. She quickly identified the silhouette of her own hand, which had been above the paper when the flash went off. But then she saw something else....

Another hand.

And unlike hers, this hand wasn't a shadow. It was translucent, enshrouded by a pale blue halo. The ghostly hand appeared to be grasping hers.

Tessa didn't realize she was crying until she tasted tears on her lips. *He's here. Watching me. Trying to touch me. So why can't I see him? Or hear him?*

Tessa transferred the photo into the stop bath but wound up with the same result—a black rectangle.

Once more, Tessa placed a blank piece of photo paper in the enlarger. This time, however, she crouched down and slid her face beneath the lens, resting her cheek on the baseboard. She closed her eyes but could still feel the quick burst of heat and light radiating from above.

Tessa quickly dropped the photo paper into the tray. She watched the dark outline of her own face appear. And then... the curves of another face began to form next to hers, its cheek pressed against hers. The face—opaque, radiating an aura of otherworldly colors—wore an expression of intense longing. She had seen this face many times before. In fact, she had studied and memorized every contour of it.

Tessa was staring at Skylar's face.

From the living room sofa, Mel called out to her. "Whoa, whoa! Where do you think you're going?"

Tessa was panting as she reached for the SUV's keys, which were dangling on a hook in the foyer. "To see a friend," she answered.

"At *this* hour? It's past ten. What happened to doctor's orders and taking it easy?"

"I'm fine, Mel."

Sitting next to Mel, Vickie chimed in. "You promised me you were going to eat something."

"I'll grab something on the way."

Mel's voice grew harsher. "Tess, whoever you need to see, it can wait till morning. Now, put the keys down and put something in your stomach."

Yet another face-off.

"I said put the keys down!" he yelled.

Tessa hurled the car keys against the wall. "Fine! I'll walk!"

She pushed through the front door and turned down the street. If Mel or Vickie tried to physically stop her, she was prepared to make a scene in front of all the neighbors. She'd done it before and was happy to do it again.

"Tessa?"

She turned and saw Vickie hurrying after her, holding the car keys in one hand and a gray hoodie in the other. "Just tell me the truth," she implored. "Where are you going?"

Tessa took the keys from Vickie but not the hoodie. "Somewhere safe. I promise."

It was well past visiting hours when Tessa emerged from the hospital's elevator, but she didn't care. Let them try and stop her. She'd throw a fit here, too. When she rushed past the nurses' station, Jasmine popped up from behind it. "Tessa? What are you doing here—?"

"I have to talk to Doris," Tessa answered.

"Hang on a sec," Jasmine said.

But Tessa didn't stop. She kept moving briskly down the hallway, even as Jasmine called after her. "Tessa? Tessa!"

Tessa turned into Doris's hospital room but found a male orderly stripping down Doris's bed, tossing the dirty sheets into a hamper on wheels.

Jasmine appeared behind Tessa. "Her family took her home this morning. There was nothing more we could do for her."

"I need to talk to her, Jazz. Can you give me her phone number?"

Jasmine shook her head firmly. "No. I can't do that, Tessa. I could lose my job."

Tessa felt a sudden, intense stab of pain in her chest. All the excitement was catching up to her.

Jasmine could immediately see that something was wrong. "You all right?"

"Fine. I just need to eat something."

But she wasn't all right. Her heart was beating erratically, speeding up, slowing down, looping inside her chest like a sputtering engine. She felt woozy.

"Sit down," Jasmine said. "Let me check you out."

"I'm fine, Jazz."

"Girl, sit your ass down or I'm gonna call Mel and Vickie right now."

Tessa relented, dropping to the edge of the bare mattress. Jasmine pulled out her stethoscope and began to listen to her heart. "Now, tell me. . . . Why do you need to see Doris so bad?"

"It has something to do with what she told me. About the afterlife. She said it's not some imaginary place in the clouds. She said it's real. And that people can reach out to us from there."

Jasmine chuckled to herself. "And I thought that old coot was crazy." She unplugged the stethoscope from her ears. "Your heartbeat's fast, but it sounds strong."

"What do you mean, you thought Doris was crazy? Did she say something to you?"

Jasmine nodded. "Believe it or not, she told me you'd be

back looking for her. Matter of fact, she left something for you. Come with me."

At the nurses' station, Jasmine pulled something from her desk drawer and handed it to Tessa. It was Doris's first book, *No More Goodbyes*, the one she'd offered Tessa when they first talked in the garden. It was like a consolation prize, the next best thing to being able to see Doris in person.

As Tessa turned to leave, Jasmine called out to her. "Tessa? I've seen a lot of dying and grieving in my time here as a nurse. And as far as I can tell, looking back never helped anyone.... Just remember, sometimes a butterfly's just a butterfly, not a sign from heaven."

It took Tessa three hours to read Doris's book cover to cover. On nearly every page, she underlined something she found relevant. Before long, she began scribbling notes and questions on a pad. It was like she was working on a school project.

Afterward, Tessa went online, visiting a myriad of websites devoted to the afterlife. Some of the websites and blogs seemed legit, while others seemed like the work of conspiracy theorists and freaks. One man claimed to be in direct contact with Abraham Lincoln. A woman insisted she'd been contacted by Lizzie Borden, the famous ax murderer, who swore she did not kill her parents and demanded a trial by jury to clear her name.

After hours of research, Tessa's biggest question was: How long? How long did disembodied spirits linger after death?

Every religion and philosophy had a different answer. The Buddhists believed a soul survived for forty-nine days after its material death. In Jewish tradition, the intermissive period lasted only thirty days, which meant that Skylar was already gone. But that made no sense because he'd contacted her the night before.

Tessa yearned for the kind of clear answers that science could provide. But everything she read were theories and conjecture. In the end, Tessa was left with more questions than answers.

sixty-
one
days
before

IT WAS PAST FIVE WHEN TESSA SPOTTED SKYLAR WALKING UP the beach. He and another lifeguard were balancing a Margate City rowboat on their shoulders. Skylar was wearing board shorts, the kind favored by surfers. His legs, sculpted from years of rowing, jutted out like granite tree trunks, and his face was sun-kissed from a long day on the lifeguard stand.

Tessa called out to him. "Skylar?"

At first, she saw a flash of excitement in his expression. But that was immediately replaced by a look of displeasure that seemed to be saying: *What the hell are* you *doing here?* Maybe Shannon was right. Maybe an email apology would have been better?

As Skylar walked past her, he said, "Give me a minute."

She nodded silently, watching him and the other lifeguard

move toward some wooden pillars beside the lifeguard shack, where they hooked both ends of the boat onto two separate pullies. Now on opposite sides of the hull, Skylar and the other lifeguard cranked their respective winches, lifting the boat off the ground until it hung three feet above the sand. When they were done, the boat was swaying back and forth like the pendulum in a grandfather clock.

Skylar and the other lifeguard high-fived and said goodbye. Skylar stood in place for a few seconds, his head tilted slightly back, as if he needed to prepare himself for what was to come. Then he walked over to Tessa.

"What's up," he said, his voice uncharacteristically emotionless. He did not remove his mirrored sunglasses, so Tessa was looking at two distorted reflections of her own face.

"I don't know what to say," Tessa said.

"Yes you do," Skylar replied firmly.

It was disconcerting to see Skylar acting so coldly. Tessa remained silent. She heard the distant rumble of the surf and the squawk of seagulls wheeling in the air above them. Her heart was racing, and she still could not find the words.

"This might be the worst apology I've ever heard," Skylar said.

Tessa couldn't help it. She burst out laughing. She could see that Skylar wanted to laugh, too, but he fought the urge. He was not ready to forgive her.

"I'm really sorry," she said. "There's no other way to say it: I totally messed up."

"What the hell happened to you?"

"I don't know," she said.

"Sorry, but that's not good enough."

"I guess it was just... too much pressure."

"Meeting my grandfather?"

"Pressure about *us*."

"What pressure?" Skylar asked. "From the first moment we met in the movie theater, I felt like I've known you my whole life."

"Exactly. We had an amazing time. And then that epic date. It felt like a lot to live up to. I was suddenly worried, what if I messed it all up?"

"In other words, you were so scared of messing it up...that you *did* mess it up?"

"I know it doesn't make sense. I just froze. Like...stage fright."

Skylar tilted up his sunglasses, sweeping his curls away from his forehead. His green eyes were sparkling and clear. "You could have at least called," he said.

"You're right. I should have. But after I chickened out, I was *so* embarrassed. Each day that went by, it felt harder to reach out.... If you knew what I've been through in my life, you'd understand why I sometimes get like this."

"Maybe you need to tell me about it?"

"I will," Tessa said. "Soon."

She watched his face. Something inside told her to touch him, so she took his hand into hers, intertwining their fingers.

She could feel the crunchy granules of sand on his palm. "If you forgive me—and let me make it up to you—I promise I won't do anything like that again. I swear."

"It's not *me* you have to make it up to. It's my grandfather."

"I'll do whatever it takes."

"Do you like dancing?" he asked.

"Dancing?"

Skylar smiled. "You'll see."

sixty-
one
days
before

SKYLAR'S GRANDFATHER MIKE LIVED IN A MUSHROOM-COLORED house in the center of Margate. He was an eccentric man who only loved to do a few things: cook, listen to baseball games on the radio, and most of all, dance. He was a wonderful dancer who had honed his craft through years of practice, starting with his first lesson when he was a boy.

Sadly, dancing was getting trickier for Mike, thanks to his macular degeneration. The vision loss started after his wife of thirty-nine years, Skylar's grandmother, died of leukemia. At first, Mike thought the problems with his eyes were caused by grief. "I don't want to see the world without her," he would say in between bouts of crying. But when Mike's vision continued to decline, Skylar's mom took him to a specialist in

Philadelphia who gave them the bad news. Mike had a progressive eye disease for which there was no cure.

Five years later, Mike had lost 80 percent of his vision, which qualified him as legally blind. He had no choice but to adjust to this new reality. For starters, he changed the layout of his furniture so he wouldn't bump into things. He attached braille dots to his pantry items so he wouldn't mix up the salt with the sugar. And he had an aide named Rosaria visit him once a week to bring groceries and audiobooks from the library.

Before Tessa came over for dinner, Skylar warned her to prepare for a performance. "He loves to dance. It's the thing that keeps him going." And true to Skylar's word, as soon as they finished dessert, Mike led Tessa and Skylar from the dining room to the living room.

Tessa was fascinated by how easily Mike was able to navigate his house without a cane. Skylar explained that Mike had lived in the house for more than thirty years and had instinctually memorized the location of every wall, every doorway, and every cabinet knob.

In the living room, Mike ordered Skylar and Tessa to sit on the sofa, which he called "a love seat." He rolled up the Persian rug that covered the floor, pushing the tube of wool against the wall. Then he pressed *Play* on the kiwi-colored cassette player sitting on the mantel.

Instantly, a chorus of horns blasted out of the tiny speakers.

It was an old swing song, the kind of music that people in the 1940s listened to. It was their version of hip-hop.

Mike began to dance. He was shockingly graceful for a man of seventy, and Tessa could see the delight in his expression as he went through his routine, a combination of tap and eccentric jazz moves. Skylar sat beside Tessa on the sofa, holding her hand while stealing glances at her reaction.

At first, Tessa was worried about Mike crashing into furniture or knocking things over. But he seemed to have an intuitive spatial awareness of his surroundings. At no point did he seem disoriented or in danger of hurting himself. Before long, she was simply enjoying the show.

Just then, Skylar's cell phone rang. He glanced down at the screen. "It's my dad," he said.

"Take it," Tessa said. "I'll be fine."

Skylar gave her a peck on the cheek, then went into the kitchen for privacy. When Tessa turned back to Mike, his hand was outstretched toward her. "Come on, little lady," he shouted. "You haven't lived until you've mamboed!"

Tessa wasn't really keen on dancing. Truth was, she was still stuffed from Mike's roast beef and potatoes. But she wanted to be polite, so she rose from the sofa and took her place beside him on the makeshift dance floor.

"Okay," Mike said. "Follow my lead. . . . Left foot forward . . . left foot back . . . then pause."

Tessa mirrored his moves with her left foot.

"Now," Mike continued, "same thing with the right leg… Right foot forward, right foot back, pause."

Tessa picked up the steps quickly. Before long, Mike pulled her closer and they began to mambo together.

"I can hear your footsteps on the floor. You have perfect timing," he said, cheering her on.

"Only because I have the best dance partner," Tessa replied playfully.

When the song came to an end, Mike released Tessa and stood still on the hardwood floor, out of breath. There was a buoyant smile on his face. Clearly ready to sit, Mike reached behind his back, fumbling for the arm of his lounge chair.

"I got you," Tessa said, clutching his elbow and guiding him into his chair. "Do you need anything else, Mike? Some water, maybe?"

"No. Please. Sit." He gestured to the sofa and she sat back down.

There was a silence as Mike continued to pant, like an old dog returning from a long walk.

"Sorry again about last week," Tessa said. "I swear, I'm not a flake."

Mike waved his hand through the air. "Forget it. I told Skylar the only girls worth falling for are the spicy ones." With that, Mike pointed to a spot over the fireplace. Tessa's eyes followed his finger to an enormous black-and-white photograph hanging on the wall. It was of Mike's late wife, her wedding photo. She was dressed in a satin ivory gown that seemed to be melting over the curves of her body.

"She was stunning," Tessa said.

There was a flash of pride on Mike's face. "I always tell people *she* was the reason I went blind. All those years looking at that gorgeous gal. Too much beauty for one set of eyes."

"You must miss her so much."

"Are you familiar with E. E. Cummings?"

"The poet?" Tessa asked.

"Yes. Very good. E. E. Cummings once described grief as a war between remembering and forgetting."

Before Tessa could respond, she heard Skylar's raised voice stray out of the kitchen. She could not understand what he was saying, but he sounded agitated. When Tessa turned back to Mike, she could see he was disturbed.

"The divorce has been tough on him," he said.

"*Divorce?*" Tessa said with surprise. "He never said anything about a divorce. He told me they were working things out."

"They haven't officially filed yet. I think they're trying to ease Skylar into it."

"I don't understand. If they don't want to be together, why would Skylar want them to be?"

"That's a good question," Mike said. "Think of it this way: When you grow up with parents who don't get along, that's how you expect relationships to be. But when you grow up the way Skylar did, with parents who were high school sweethearts and had a great big love affair, well, can you blame him for expecting only sunshine and rainbows?"

Tessa was suddenly reminded of the first conversation they'd had in the movie theater. She believed that the most memorable love stories ended sadly. Skylar did not. And now Tessa knew why.

"Many people don't realize there's a price you pay for love," Mike said.

"Oh?" Tessa asked. "What is it?"

Mike smirked. "I'm afraid that's something we all have to learn for ourselves."

Skylar returned to the living room. The smile on his face seemed unusually forced, as though he didn't want Tessa and Mike to know that he was upset.

"Everything okay?" Tessa asked.

"Yeah. All good."

Mike rose to his feet. "Well, as much as I'd love to chum around with you kids, this old fart needs some sleep. You two have a wonderful night." As he turned to leave, Mike wagged a finger of warning. "No funny business. Okay?"

Skylar smiled. "Good night, Grandpa."

After Mike shuffled off to his bedroom, Tessa asked Skylar, *"Funny business?"*

"He doesn't want us hooking up," Skylar answered.

Defying his grandfather's warning, Skylar nudged Tessa onto her back and lay down next to her, slipping his arms and legs through hers. They made out for several minutes, stopping only when they needed to catch their breaths.

"He's awesome, isn't he?" Skylar asked.

"God, yeah. You're so lucky to have him in your life."

"He's given me so much perspective. He's seen so many ups and downs. And despite the setbacks, he still has a passion to live. That's how I want to be."

By now, Tessa was feeling the urge to ask Skylar about the argument he'd had with his father. But Skylar had already read her expression. "Did the call with my dad upset you?"

"How come you didn't tell me your parents were getting a divorce?"

Skylar shrugged. "How come you won't let me see your photos?"

"We're not talking about me right now."

Skylar sat up and rubbed his face with his hands. His head drooped over the back rim of the sofa. He was now staring up at the ceiling. He remained silent.

"You know," Tessa said, "just because they're splitting up doesn't mean they don't care about each other. It only means—"

"It means they've given up. And I don't think that's fair."

"Fair to who? Them? Or you?"

Skylar lifted his head and straightened his posture, as if he was preparing to say something important. "When you're rowing in a race and you reach the last twenty meters, that's when your body starts to fail. Every single muscle inside you is burning with pain, your lungs are begging for oxygen, and all the cells in your body are screaming for you to quit. . . . But if you want to win, that's the moment you have to dig deeper and row harder. You have to make the pain your friend. That's the only way to win the race. And that's the only way they'll save their marriage."

Tessa was touched by Skylar's innocence, by his naive devotion to the purity of love. It was not an act. He was a true believer.

"You think I'm delusional," he said.

"No," Tessa replied, sweeping some curls away from his forehead. "But you *do* sound like someone who's never been hurt in life."

"Like you have?"

"I'm not pretending to be some kind of hero. But I *have* experienced a ton of shit."

"You ever gonna tell me about it?" Skylar asked.

"Soon," Tessa assured him. "But right now, this girl would love—and I mean *love*—a scoop of double chocolate chip ice cream. And a walk on the beach."

"Your wish," Skylar said, "is my command."

thirty-
five
days
after

"THE BARDO?"

Tessa and Shannon were standing outside the school's gymnasium, waiting to sign in for Saturday morning's SAT exam. Shannon was paging through Doris's book.

"There are a lot of different names for it," Tessa said. "But that's what the Buddhists call it. It's the place we all go after we die."

"Not me," Shannon said. "I'm goin' to Jamaica."

"It's like this waiting room for our souls. After we die, our souls separate from our bodies, and we spend a bunch of time in this intermediate state before we move on to...whatever's next."

"*A bunch of time?*"

"It's not really scientific. Some souls linger for weeks, others stay for months or even years. It's different for every soul."

"Okay, and you think Skylar's reaching out to you from this...waiting room?"

"They were color photos, Shannon! You know I don't shoot in color. I don't even have the chemicals to develop it!"

"But you can't show me the photos because...?"

"I told you. The stop bath didn't work. I don't know why. Maybe spirits can't be captured on film?"

"Right," Shannon said sarcastically.

They reached the sign-in desk. Gerald was sitting behind it, and upon seeing Tessa, he perked up and pushed a pen toward her. "H-hey, Tessa. I, uh, seated you at desk fifty-four, right beneath the AC vent. It can get really warm in there."

Tessa signed her name. "Thanks, Gerald."

As they moved off, Shannon quipped: "It pays to have friends in high places."

They entered the gymnasium. There were a hundred desks arranged in a checkerboard pattern, all of them numbered. The murmur of chatting students echoed off the ceiling. So did the squeaking of everyone's sneakers on the parquet floor.

Tessa trailed behind Shannon, continuing to press her about what had happened in the darkroom. "What if 'dying' and coming back changed me? What if...I don't know...it tuned me to another frequency?"

"You mean the dead-people frequency?"

Frustrated, Tessa threw her hands up.

"I'm sorry, Tess," Shannon said. "I want to believe you, I swear. But...messages from the other side?"

The test monitor cupped his hands around his mouth and screamed out into the gymnasium: "Two-minute warning!"

Shannon located her desk and turned to Tessa. "Tess? I love you like a sister. But I don't think this is about color photos or waiting rooms or bardos."

"Okay, fine. Then what's it about?"

Shannon handed Doris's book back to Tessa. "A girl who doesn't want to let go."

Tessa breezed through the reading and vocabulary sections, but then came the math portion. What Kryptonite was to Superman, algebra was to Tessa. It was like a part of her brain shut down when she looked at graphs or triangles or numbers. After ten minutes, she already needed a break. She put down her pencil and rubbed her temples with her fingers, making small circles to relieve the tension. She wondered whether it might be best to walk out of the room and forget the test altogether.

But then she thought about the promise she'd made to Skylar. He'd been unyielding in his belief that Tessa not only had the talent to get into art school but that she'd be offered a scholarship from every college she applied to. Throughout the summer, they'd had several conversations—and one argument—over Tessa's future plans. He couldn't understand why Tessa wouldn't even *consider* college. *What do you have to lose?* he'd wondered.

Tessa eventually agreed to take the SATs. And now here she was, adrift in a sea of trigonometry, fulfilling her promise to him.

At that moment, Tessa heard the sound of her pencil rolling. It lasted barely a second. She looked down and discovered her pencil had moved a few inches. Its tip was now pointing to the answer *b*.

Intrigued, Tessa slid the pencil back to where it had been. Immediately, it rolled to *b* again—*on its own*. Tessa released a gleeful laugh that drew the stares of several students around her. She turned red with embarrassment and looked back down. Then picked up her pencil and filled in the tiny circle next to *b*.

At that moment, Tessa felt something touch her. At first, it was gentle, like a soft breeze grazing her elbow. But then the sensation intensified. It now felt like . . . invisible fingers clutching her wrist. Something—or someone—had taken hold of her hand.

Rather than fighting it, Tessa released herself to the touch. The force nudged her hand down to the next answer on the test and prompted her to fill in the circle next to the letter *c*.

Skylar's helping me take the test!

It was a strange feeling to watch her own hand, without any guidance, travel down the test page and rapidly color in answers: *d—c—b—a—c*.

Ten minutes later, Tessa had completed the math section of her SATs. But strangely, Skylar wasn't done. The invisible force shoved her hand to the top of the test sheet, prompting her to fill in more bubbles. She was now answering the same questions a second, then a third time. How could a math question have three answers?

A few minutes later, the force released its grip on her arm. Tessa was now staring down at a test sheet that would undoubtedly be voided.

But then Tessa noticed something.... The bubbles...the ones she had filled in. They weren't random. They formed letters. Tessa spun the test sheet on her desk ninety degrees so that it looked like a tiny movie screen. And now Tessa could read the message that Skylar had sent her:

5 DAYS LEFT

Her insides began fluttering uncontrollably—and it took all of Tessa's effort not to shriek out in manic joy. Skylar had just answered the question that had been nagging her since she'd read Doris's book. Now Tessa knew, without a doubt, that Skylar's spirit would linger on earth for only five more days. After that, any hope of seeing him one last time would be lost forever.

Just then, a neighboring student's cell phone began to ring, shattering the silence in the gymnasium. The test monitor was livid. "Cell phone use is prohibited during the test!" he hollered.

As the student fumbled to mute his phone, Tessa heard

something else. Another ringtone. And then another. And another. It was the most amazing thing she'd ever witnessed. A hundred phones, all of them ringing at the same time, like a digital chorus.

But that wasn't the strangest part. The strangest part was that every single ringtone was playing the same song, *their* song.

> *More than this, you know there's nothing...*
> *More than this, tell me one thing...*

Tessa's eyes traced the crowd and found Shannon. She, too, was holding her own ringing phone. With shock on her face, Shannon locked eyes with Tessa, her expression sending a wordless message: *I believe you.*

fifty-
eight
days
before

SKYLAR SAID TO MEET HIM ON THE BEACH AFTER HIS SHIFT ended, at six sharp. He reminded Tessa to bring her camera, a reminder she definitely didn't need, since she brought it everywhere. It was like an appendage, as much a part of her as her arms or legs.

The beach was unusually quiet, with only a few clusters of people still lying on the sand. It was the Fourth of July, and most of the beachgoers had left early to attend barbecues or watch the annual fireworks display.

When Tessa arrived at the lifeguard stand, she was surprised to find Shannon and Judd sitting on the perch, sharing a pair of earbuds—one in her right ear, one in his left ear. They were bopping their heads to a song.

Through grit and determination, Shannon had succeeded

in her quest and had been spending time with Judd since the end of the school year. But much to Shannon's chagrin, they'd only fooled around once. Nothing had advanced, at least not physically, in the past few weeks.

"What are *you* guys doing here?" Tessa asked.

"Skylar texted me and said to be here at six," Shannon answered. "Said he had a surprise."

"He sent me the exact same text," Judd added.

Behind them, there was a savage rumbling sound. It was a beach patrol vehicle, a gargantuan 4x4 with jumbo tires and spinning police lights on top. It was barreling toward them, kicking up sheets of sand. Tessa spotted Skylar behind the wheel, mirrored sunglasses on. Damn, he was cute.

Skylar parked the jeep and jumped to the sand. "What up, kids?" He threw his arms around Tessa, and she felt a flurry of kisses on her neck. Wrapped inside his embrace, she felt... secure. No. That wasn't the word. *Home.* The safest place in the world. With a roof over her head that kept the cold out and the warm in.

"So what's the big surprise?" Shannon asked.

"Jump into the truck—you're about to find out," Skylar said.

Judd leaped off the lifeguard stand and landed with a soft thud in the sand. He didn't offer to help Shannon down. "Don't worry," Shannon cracked. "I'll manage."

She followed Judd into the back seat of the truck and shut the door, crossing her arms petulantly.

As Tessa moved to climb into the passenger seat, Skylar

stopped her. He dangled the keys before her eyes. "Wanna drive?"

Tessa flashed a devious look and snatched the keys from Skylar. "You're gonna regret this."

Tessa drove like a madwoman. She sped up and down the width of the beach, doing doughnuts, blasting the siren, and zigzagging with reckless abandon. In the back seat, Shannon and Judd were tossed around like they were on an amusement park ride.

"You need to slow your bitch ass down!" Shannon screamed.

In retaliation, Tessa swerved the jeep onto the shoreline, spraying ocean water through the windows, drenching Shannon.

"NOT COOL!" Shannon shouted. "NOT! COOL! AT! ALL!"

Skylar tapped Tessa's shoulder. "Pull up over there." He directed her to an empty parking lot, its asphalt dusted with a thin layer of sand. Tessa pulled the beast to a stop and heaved the gear into *Park*.

In back, Shannon released an overly dramatic sigh of relief. "Praise the Lord."

"Somebody won their driver's license in a sweepstakes," Judd said.

Tessa cut the engine and turned to Skylar. "Okay, we made it. Now, what's the big surprise?"

Before Skylar could answer, a flash of blinding white light flooded through the windshield, startling everyone. The truck began trembling, even though the engine was off. Tessa heard a rapid thudding sound from above. She looked up and spotted the Margate City Beach Patrol helicopter descending from the sky. It landed a hundred feet in front of the jeep, its whirling blades kicking up litter and sand.

"Grab your camera," Skylar said. "We're going for a little ride."

Tessa released a loud, joyous shriek. She had mentioned several times to Skylar that it was her dream to take some aerial photos of the island at sunset, but the flight had always been too costly. Only that was the thing about Skylar. He never gave up. He always found a way.

Tessa leaped from the driver's seat and landed on the pavement. She instantly felt the powerful rush of air from the helicopter. She noticed Shannon was still in the back seat, staying put. Tessa heaved herself up onto the truck's footrest. She spoke to Shannon through the open window.

"You're not coming?" she asked.

"I can't," Shannon said. "I get airsick."

Airsick? What the hell was she talking about? Shannon didn't get airsick. She and her family flew to more exotic locations than anyone she knew.

It only took a moment for Tessa to realize that Shannon, like always, had a master plan. After all, she was in the back seat of a gigantic truck with her crush, and there was more than enough space for them to hook up.

Ever the loyal friend, Tessa played along. "Oh yeah, I

forgot." She turned to Judd, who looked disheartened. "Maybe you two should stay behind and..."

"Keep an eye on the truck?" Shannon finished.

"Great idea," Tessa said.

Up in the air, the sky was a dome of dark blue. Tessa took photos as quickly as she could. Every second presented hundreds of options, but she could only click so fast. The pilot, Jack, didn't notice when she unhooked her seat belt and leaned across Skylar's legs so she could take photos out the other side, too.

"Gah!" Tessa cursed. "I didn't bring my telephoto lens!"

Far in the distance, the annual Atlantic City fireworks display had just begun. Thin streamers of light were rocketing off a barge, exploding into the sky, releasing fountains of colorful embers that faded as they fell toward the sea.

Tessa pointed to the fireworks. "Hey, Jack! Think you could fly us through it?"

Jack replied with the cockiness of his former military pilot self. "Did three tours in Afghanistan. I think I can handle a bunch of Roman candles."

Skylar interjected. "Hold on a second. Isn't that a little bit... insane?"

"I told you," Tessa said. "I'll do anything for a good photo."

Conceding, Skylar nodded to Jack, who pushed the control stick to the left and abruptly banked the helicopter, causing Tessa's stomach to flutter. As they drew closer to the fireworks,

Tessa could start to feel shock waves penetrating the Plexiglas windows, rippling through the insides of her body. All her senses were aflame.

As they entered the eye of the fireworks display, Tessa lowered her camera and pulled Skylar's arms around her torso, crossing them over her heart. Embers were exploding around them, ricocheting off the helicopter's windows like a swarm of glowing insects.

Skylar placed his chin on Tessa's shoulder and pressed the side of his face against hers. She felt his stubble on her cheek and could smell the sea in his hair.

Tessa turned around, and her lips found Skylar's. The taste of his mouth was faintly sweet. She could no longer tell the difference between the fireworks outside and the ones inside her heart. The moment was so astoundingly perfect that Tessa spoke without thinking. "You almost make me believe in happy endings."

fifty
days
before

From the day Tessa persuaded Mel to let her convert the attic into a darkroom, no one was allowed in, not even Shannon. It was her most sacred space—more private than her bedroom, her school locker, even the diary she periodically scribbled her thoughts into. To make her feelings clear to everyone, Tessa had hung a handwritten sign on the door that read I'D TURN AROUND IF I WERE YOU.

But after two months of dating Skylar, Tessa could no longer keep him out. He hadn't been overly aggressive about his desire to see it—that wasn't his style. But he *did* make it clear, numerous times, that he wanted to see her work space and, more important, *he wanted to see her work.* "How can I ever know who you are if you won't show me the thing you love most?"

On the drive home from the helicopter ride, Skylar had casually mentioned that he'd love to watch her develop the photos she'd just taken. Tessa, still buzzing from the flight, had surprised herself by saying yes.

The following Friday, after his shift ended, Skylar showed up at Tessa's house. She kissed him at the front door and brushed the sand from his hair. Then she led him upstairs into her darkroom.

"I can't believe you're finally letting me into the inner sanctum," he said excitedly.

"If you tell anyone, I'll disavow all knowledge of it. Then poison you."

Tessa spent the next hour showing Skylar the entire process of developing a roll of film, starting with the negatives, moving to the enlarger, the developing chemicals, and finally, hanging the prints on a clothesline to dry.

Skylar was mostly silent throughout the process, only asking a few questions. He seemed much more interested in Tessa's photos, which were everywhere—piled in stacks on the floor, tacked onto the walls, and dangling from wires that zigzagged across the attic like power lines. At one point, while Tessa was developing a photo of the helicopter pilot, she discovered that Skylar was no longer standing next to her. He'd moved off and found her portfolio, which he was paging through.

Not even Mr. Duffy knew that Tessa had secretly assembled a collection of her best photos. The truth was, it had less to do with Mr. Duffy's steady pressure and more to do with Skylar. He was going to Brown—an Ivy League school. How could Tessa expect him to respect her if she had no ambitions, no plan for her future? At the minimum, she needed to go through the motions so Skylar didn't think she was a total washout. So she'd spent the past month culling her photos, assembling the best ones in the leather book that Vickie had bought her last Christmas.

"I thought I told you no touching," Tessa said sharply.

"If you didn't want me to see it, why'd you leave it out?"

"Good point," Tessa said. She nodded for him to keep going.

He turned the pages, studying each image carefully. There were photos from every nook and cranny of the island she called home. The beach. The bay. City streets. And of course, several photos from inside the Empyrean, including a close-up of the words YOU ARE ENTERING THE LAND OF LOVE. There was even a shot of Skylar, the one of him crossing the finish line on the day he and Tessa were reunited.

When Skylar saw the photo of the cell-phone tower, Tessa anticipated his confusion. "It's a—"

"Cell-phone tower," Skylar finished. "It's an allegory, right? While we go about our daily lives, technology coopts our most prized totems. Even nature."

Tessa felt a burst of adoration for the boy standing before her. It was as if someone had handed him the instruction manual to her mind. He just...knew. Tessa rose onto her toes and kissed Skylar on the side of his face.

"What was that for?" he asked.

"For saying it way better than I ever could."

She slipped the photo out of the book and handed it to him. "I want you to have it."

"Really?"

"Really," she said.

He took the photo, seeming to understand how big a gesture this was. "Tess, I know you hate compliments, but seriously, this work...*your* work...it's unbelievable. It's like... you see things that no one else does."

"Shows how much you know about photography," she replied.

"Hey, I'm being serious—you could sell this stuff."

"Maybe on Etsy."

Tessa saw a flash of frustration in Skylar's eyes. It was the same expression everyone made when she refused their compliments. How could she make him understand the contradiction that existed in her heart? That she desperately wanted his approval, yet detested herself for wanting it, because it implied an emotional need she was too scared to acknowledge.

"I don't know why you always put yourself down," he said. "If you're not going to be on your own side, who will?"

"You," Tessa said with a smirk.

Skylar cradled her face, kissing her. Tessa pulled him closer, guiding his hand beneath her shirt. As they kissed more deeply and his hand swam over the curves of her chest, Tessa felt something completely unfamiliar.... She felt pretty. Gone was the usual impulse to hide her body. In that moment, if Skylar wanted to unbutton her jeans, she'd let him. Losing her virginity on the floor of her most sacred space made all the sense in the world.

But Skylar surprised her by stepping back. On his face, he wore the expression of someone who'd stumbled onto an ancient secret. "I just realized something," he said. "Something that's missing from every single one of your photos."

Tessa sighed. "Yeah, I know. Color."

"No," he replied. "*You.*"

"Me?"

"Yeah. Unless I missed it, I don't see a single self-portrait of you in here."

"Right. Just what the world needs, another selfie," Tessa quipped. "A photographer should point her lens outward, at the world, so she can dissect and understand it."

"What's wrong with trying to dissect and understand yourself?"

Tessa considered Skylar's question. The only way to answer it truthfully would be to tell him everything. It would be the equivalent of dropping a nuclear bomb onto their relationship. But Skylar had earned the right to know.

"Let's take a walk," she said.

The air outside was damp and thick with the smell of bay water. Skylar held Tessa's hand as they walked the streets of

Margate, passing beneath pools of amber streetlight that dotted the town's sidewalks.

The moment they stepped outside, Tessa had second thoughts. Revealing the details of her childhood would probably change everything—and not for the better. Sure, Skylar might *pretend* to be sympathetic. But then his behavior would change. He'd look at her differently, treat her differently. She'd resent him for that and get combative. From there, it was only a matter of time before their relationship crashed and burned.

"I never met my real father," Tessa began. "He ran off before I was born. And my mom...God, my mom...The charitable way to describe her would be...flaky."

"That bad?" Skylar asked.

"Let's put it this way. When I was a little girl, instead of counting sheep to go to sleep, I'd count her fiancés."

"And Mel was one of them?"

"Mel was the last one. The final victim before Mom ghosted us all for good."

"You mean, you never heard from her again?"

Tessa shook her head. "Not even a postcard. She could be dead for all I know."

"So, is that when Mel took you in?"

"No, that's when he *tried* to take me in. But the law mandated that I reside with a blood relative, so they sent me to live with my grandma Pat. Unfortunately, she was extremely sick by then. I was only ten years old but helped take care of her.

One morning, I walked into her bedroom with her coffee, and her eyes were frozen wide. She'd died in her sleep."

"Shit, Tessa. I'm sorry," Skylar said.

"I remember sitting there, next to her body . . . and I know this is gonna sound cruel, but . . . I didn't care that she was dead. I was too worried about where I was going to go. I had no family left."

Tessa's voice began to tremble, but she stifled the urge to cry. She did not want to be a ball of tears in front of him. It would only make what was to come that much worse.

"It was around that time," she continued, "that Mel petitioned the court again. Only the judge didn't look too kindly on a middle-aged bachelor wanting to adopt a little girl."

"Wait a second. They were worried that Mel was a creeper? *Mel?*"

Tessa chuckled. "Hysterical, right? Mel is literally the most nonsexual dude in the universe. He won't even come upstairs if I'm taking a shower."

"Okay. So if you didn't move in with Mel, where'd you go?"

Tessa braced herself. "Family services," she said.

She could tell that Skylar wasn't sure what that meant. Truth was, most people didn't.

"*Family services* is a euphemism," she explained.

"For?"

"Foster care."

There was no change in Skylar's expression. He seemed to

take it all in without judgment. And that made Tessa feel safe enough to continue.

"I bounced around a lot. Sometimes, I'd be with a family for a year, sometimes for a few weeks. Some of the families were okay, but most were bad. A few were brutal. A lot of the time it wasn't the adults who were the problem, it was the other kids in the house. They'd get jealous and territorial. They could really hurt you."

"Physically, you mean?"

"Sometimes. But the mind games would mess you up the most. . . . Remember in the darkroom, when you said I see things that others don't?"

"Yeah."

"You're not the first person who's told me that. What no one understands is I wasn't born like this. It was an acquired skill, a survival mechanism. When you live with strangers who can hurt you, you have to observe everything. You have to notice the looks in their eyes when they come home from work. Did they have a shitty day? Is there alcohol on their breath? You have to be in a constant state of high alert, ready to adjust your behavior at a moment's notice. When you're a foster kid, you learn the hard way to . . ."

"Keep your distance?"

They locked eyes. And there was an unspoken exchange of words. Now Skylar knew. Now he knew why—even though she adored him to bits—Tessa could never get too close to him. With a past like hers, how could she ever trust anyone?

"How long were you in foster care?" Skylar asked.

"Five years, ten months, twelve days. Anyway, while all that was going on, Mel finally found himself a wife. And Vickie pushed him to try for me again. By then, Vickie was too old to have kids, so I guess she saw me as the next best thing. With a mom now in the picture, the judge changed his mind and let them take me in."

"So that's why you call them *genetic strangers*?"

"It's just a little joke of mine."

Skylar nodded silently, but Tessa sensed there was something he wanted to say.

"What?" she asked.

"The thing is, Tess . . . it doesn't come off as a joke."

"How does it come off?"

"Ungrateful."

Tessa felt a spark of anger. "That's not fair. I *do* appreciate them."

"Then how come you don't call either of them Mom or Dad?"

"Trust me. It's not a big deal."

"Maybe not to you. But sometimes . . . people need to hear the words."

"They're *not* my parents, Sky. Calling them Mom or Dad would just be a lie."

"You call the people who abandoned you Mom and Dad but not the people who took you in and gave you a loving home?"

Tessa yanked her hand away from Skylar and crossed her arms. She was mad, not because he was wrong but because he was right. That was the hardest part of being with someone who owned your instruction manual. They called you on your shit.

Tessa felt Skylar take her hand back. Against her will, her heart softened.

They walked beneath a broken streetlamp that was buzzing and flickering like a strobe. Skylar turned to her, his green eyes wide with compassion.

"Thanks for telling me, Tess."

thirty-
nine
days
before

SKYLAR WAS FRUSTRATED. THE MAP APP HAD FROZEN TEN MINutes ago and now they were definitely lost. He turned to Tessa, who was sitting beside him in the passenger seat, a picnic basket between her legs.

"Are you sure about this?" he said. "The GPS isn't showing anything."

"I told you. It's not on any map. Just keep driving," she said.

Outside the jeep's windows, the forest was dark and dense with foliage, its shadowy contours enshrouded within clouds of mist. The dirt road they were driving over was covered with fallen brush and large divots, so Skylar had to drive slowly, doing his best to navigate the hazards.

Since his first day back in Margate, Skylar had been complaining that the inlet's waterway was too choppy to train in.

There were mornings when he had to skip his rows altogether, and he began to express concern about arriving at college out of shape. Thankfully, Tessa knew the whereabouts of a lake, hidden away inside a forest that sat behind the turnpike. It was another place she had stumbled onto during one of her photo jaunts. The only problem was, Tessa had only a vague idea of where the lake was located. It was nearly six in the morning and Skylar had been driving up and down this dirt road for an hour. Tessa began to worry she may have mixed up the location of the lake.

But then, through a break in the mist, Tessa saw a clearing that looked familiar. She pointed with excitement. "Over there!"

"I see it," Skylar said, his mood lifting.

The jeep emerged from beneath a canopy of trees. The sky was still dark and studded with stars. Skylar pulled to a stop and looked out the windshield. Even though the fog was thinner here, they still couldn't yet see the whole lake, just its shoreline.

"Come on," Tessa said.

Skylar climbed out of the jeep and followed Tessa across a patch of sand. They stopped at the water's edge and took in the surroundings. The lake stretched several miles, its glassy surface still and inviting. Clusters of fireflies hung above the waterline, whirling in circles through the air, their mirror images reflected below.

Tessa noticed the way Skylar was looking at the water. He

was like a sculptor studying a piece of raw granite, seeing its potential. Without lifting his eyes from the lake, he spoke in a respectful hush, conscious not to spoil the stillness. "When a rower dies," he said, "if they've lived a moral and compassionate life, *this* is what heaven looks like."

"See, I've always imagined heaven as Paris in the rain. Wet cobblestone streets, mist in the air."

"And everything in black and white?" Skylar joked.

"Get out of my head."

"Have you ever been? To Paris?"

"Someday."

"Avec moi?"

Tessa smirked. "Could always use a translator."

"You know, my parents honeymooned there. I'm saving up to send them back for their twenty-fifth anniversary."

Tessa felt the urge to say something. "Sky? What if they don't want to go to Paris?"

"Who doesn't want to go to Paris?"

"I mean, what if they don't want to go *together*. It's not a crime to fall out of love, you know."

He turned to her, looking defiant. "Love never dies, Tessa."

Tessa realized that Skylar was so blinded by his belief in true love that he couldn't even *see* the alternative. In his mind, only happy endings were permitted.

"You don't like to let go of things, do you?" she asked.

Skylar grinned. "Ya noticed?" He gestured to his jeep. "Help me with my shell?"

Tessa followed him back to his jeep. He yanked the canvas tarp off his jeep's roof. On the rack, she saw a wooden shell along with two pairs of oars. It wasn't Skylar's usual boat. It was much longer and wider.

"What is it?" Tessa asked.

"A double shell."

"Is someone else coming?"

"Yeah. *You.*"

Tessa opened her mouth in horror. "What? No, I just want to sit here and take photos."

"Hey. You showed me what you love to do in the darkroom. Now you need to let me show you what I love to do."

How could Tessa say no?

There were so many things to remember, it was borderline overwhelming. *"Feather your blades,"* *"keep your knees together,"* *"hold your shoulders down,"* *"use your legs, not your arms."* Then there were the strange terms that she'd never heard before: *weigh enough, recovery,* and *catch.* Despite her distress, Skylar had the patience of a saint. He coached Tessa from the rear seat, offering adjustments to help her find her stroke.

Tessa wasn't sure if she'd ever get the hang of rowing. But there *was* a fleeting moment when she and Skylar harmonized their strokes, and she felt a glimmer of what it meant to be in sync with another human being. In a way, the experience made her understand Skylar more deeply. He was a person, she realized, who loved—even needed—to connect to others. It explained so much about him.

By late morning, the fog had burned off and Tessa was hungry, so they came ashore to eat lunch. They found a small patch of sand and Skylar spread an old wool blanket over it. Tessa had packed a few sandwiches and a bag of potato chips. After eating, they napped in each other's arms until the sun rose above the treetops. She was awakened by the sound of Skylar's voice, reciting a poem to her: *I know I am but summer to your heart, And not the full four seasons of the year...."*

"Is that Millay?" Tessa asked.

He stroked her face. "You always get my references."

Tessa was mindful that the poem was about a summer love...that ended.

"Cheer up," she said. "We still have a lot of time left."

"Not as much as I thought," he said sadly. "My coach asked all freshman rowers to report to practice a week earlier."

"Oh."

"Maybe," Skylar said, "we should talk about what's next?"

His question made Tessa feel oddly defensive. "I just figured you'd leave for college, get caught up in your rowing, and find someone else."

Skylar's face hardened. "Are you being serious?"

"I mean...what can we do? You'll be up there and I'll still be here."

"Only for a year. After that, we could be together again."

"How?"

"Apply to RISD."

"What—?"

"Shannon says your art teacher has an 'in' there."

"Ugh! She's got such a big mouth."

"It's the best art school in the country. And it's in Providence, the same city as Brown. If you got in, we could be together. For real. With no more ticking clock."

"Even if I could get in—which I doubt—my family can't afford it."

"With your talent, you could get a scholarship," Skylar insisted.

"Why can't we just be happy with what we have?"

Skylar sat up, his eyes wide and tender. "Because I love you, Tess."

No.

He didn't just say that, did he?

Please be a mistake.

Tessa felt a surge of anger. It was like she wanted to lash out at Skylar, pounce on him, strike him with her fists. Why did he have to complicate things by telling her he loved her? Didn't he know they were the words she *dreaded* hearing? That she had long ago accepted she was unlovable, and no one—not even Skylar—could change her mind about that?

It suddenly occurred to Tessa why she'd told Skylar about her past. It wasn't to bring him closer. It was to *push him away.* The reality of Tessa's past should have been a magnetic pole that repelled Skylar. But Tessa's plan had failed, because now he wasn't just thinking about their future; he'd used the three words that demanded a response.

A distant rumble of thunder snapped Tessa back to the lake. Skylar was staring at her, still waiting for her to say *I love you* back. But Tessa could not utter the words. To do so would risk placing her heart into the hands of another, something she had vowed never to do again.

"We should get going," Skylar said, his voice devoid of emotion. She'd never heard him sound like this. He was embarrassed and hurt.

Skylar stood up and began to secure the boat to his jeep's roof. It started to drizzle. Tessa rose to her feet and watched him, thinking how easily a single bad moment could undo hundreds of good ones.

Something stirred inside her. It was undefined at first, but it quickly took root. It was the desperate need to make Skylar understand that—even though she couldn't say the words—she *did* love him, more than anything or anyone.

She tapped him from behind, but he did not turn. "Please be patient," she said. "I'll get there. I promise."

Tessa clutched his shoulders and spun him around. She saw tears spilling down his cheeks. Her heart froze. She'd hurt him more than she realized. And yet, his vulnerability kindled something inside her, something physical. Overcome with desire, Tessa pressed her lips hungrily to his, attempting to silently transmit the three words she could not say.

Skylar seemed surprised by the force of her kiss. But he quickly responded, throwing his arms around Tessa's back, lifting her off the ground. She swung her legs up and wrapped them tightly around his waist.

Skylar lowered Tessa to the lakeshore. She felt the sand beneath her backside conforming to the curves of her body, as if the earth were making way for them.

And then it was just Skylar's green eyes staring into hers, assuring her that everything would be okay.

thirty-
six
days
after

FOUR DAYS LEFT.

It wasn't until Shannon lit the incense that Tessa realized her best friend had gone kook.

"A séance?" Tessa asked. "In *here*?"

Shannon did not respond. She was too focused on transforming her bedroom into a psychic studio. She'd already lit dozens of votive candles, placed an array of crystals on her windowsills, and hung Wiccan amulets from hooks she'd screwed into her ceiling. And of course, there was the incense. Shannon had filled several brass holders with tiny cones that were wafting the overpowering scent of patchouli into the air. At least Shannon wasn't sprinkling holy water. Not yet, anyway.

Shannon's cocker spaniel, Waffles, was whining and scratching at the door. He was desperate to escape the fumes. Tessa felt sympathy for the dog and released him, then closed the door and locked it once again.

"Why don't we just go to a real medium?" Tessa asked. "Someone who's an actual expert on communicating with the deceased?"

Shannon waved her hand dismissively. "Those people are cranks. Besides, Skylar didn't need a medium to visit you those other times."

Tessa noticed a stack of New Age books on Shannon's desk. They had ridiculous titles like *Hello From Heaven*, *We Do Not Die*, and *Enjoy Your Own Funeral*.

Tessa chuckled. *"Enjoy Your Own Funeral?"*

"It happens to be a classic of the metaphysical-paranormal genre."

"You read it?"

"Of course. I read them all."

"You read *all* these books? In *one* night?"

"Bitch, speed-reading's my superpower."

It warmed Tessa's heart to know that, thanks to the gymnasium incident, her best friend had joined her quest.

Shannon flipped the light switch, and the room went dark. The two of them sat on the carpet, cross-legged, their knees pressed against each other. Shannon took Tessa's hands into hers and closed her eyes. Then she began speaking in a tone of seriousness that was unusual for Shannon.

"We begin this invocation by asking archangel Michael to protect us from any malevolent spirits that may be seeking a gateway to the earthbound sphere."

Tessa was so impressed, she blurted out, "You wrote that?"

Shannon's eyes opened with annoyance. "You're interrupting my invocation."

"Right, sorry."

After finishing the invocation, Shannon reached under her bed and slid out a large blank pad, which she balanced on their knees. On top of the pad, she placed a heart-shaped piece of wood that had script carved into its surface. Tessa wasn't certain, but the letters looked like Sanskrit or maybe Arabic.

"Is it a Ouija board?" Tessa asked.

Shannon rolled her eyes, like a teacher who'd just been asked a stupid question by a student. "Please. It's a *planchette*. There's a pencil tip attached to the bottom. We ask questions and Skylar's spirit communicates by moving our hands to write messages, just like he did in the gym yesterday."

She had to give Shannon credit—she'd definitely thought this out.

"Come on, now," Shannon ordered. "Fingertips down."

Tessa lowered her fingers to the wooden planchette. It was cold to the touch. She looked across at Shannon, whose eyelids were closed again.

Shannon tilted her head back and spoke into the air. "Skylar? I sit here with the mortal shell known as Tessa Jacobs. She seeks to communicate with you. Can you hear us?"

Almost instantly, Tessa felt the planchette shift beneath her fingers. "It moved!" she cried out.

"Sorry," Shannon said. "That was me."

Tessa sighed, her excitement quelled. She returned her fingers to the planchette and Shannon resumed. "Skylar? Are you here? If you are, can you tell us why you're reaching out to Tessa?"

The planchette remained motionless.

"Maybe he needs to hear *my* voice?" Tessa said.

"Good call."

Tessa looked up into the air, her throat straining with emotion. "Sky? It's Tess.... Can you hear me? Can you tell me what you want?"

She looked down, but the planchette did not move, not even a little.

After a half hour of one-sided conversation, Tessa was prepared to give up. But Shannon wasn't easily discouraged.

She ordered Tessa to sit on a stool and stare into a mirror hung on the back of her closet door. "It's called scrying," Shannon explained. "The deceased use the mirror as a gateway to the living. All you have to do is look into the mirror in a trancelike state."

Trancelike state? Tessa wasn't really sure what that meant, so she improvised. She spent the next half hour staring at her own face, counting her breaths—in through the nose, out through the mouth.... *In...out...in...out...*

Tessa was beginning to feel light-headed. But worse than

that was the appearance of her face. She knew that the lack of food and sleep were taking their toll on her. But here, in front of the mirror, it was impossible not to be startled by the vacant reflection staring back at her. *Where did I go? Am I really that pale, that sickly-looking?* If Skylar was going to appear behind this mirror, he ought to come right now, before she entered a spiral of self-loathing. Sadly, Skylar did not appear.

But Shannon still wasn't ready to quit. She had one more idea. She led Tessa downstairs into her living room and sat her across from the family's massive flat-screen TV. Shannon turned it on and switched the channel to static. "It's called instrumental trans-communication," she said. "Skylar can use the TV monitor as a bridge to our world."

Staring at static wasn't easy. Tessa began to hallucinate. She saw amorphous shapes and pulsing tentacles of light. There was a fleeting moment when she thought she saw the faintest outline of a face, but it quickly dissolved into a dance of blue-and-white static. No matter how long Tessa stared, she could not see Skylar. The bridge between their worlds, it seemed, was closed for repairs.

Tessa flopped onto her back. Shannon dropped down next to her. They lay side by side on the carpet, both of them defeated.

"Maybe...," Shannon said, "I should have read more books?"

"Shan, just the fact that you believe me means *so* much."

A thought suddenly popped into Tessa's head. It was

something she'd sensed unconsciously each time Skylar's spirit had contacted her. But it was only now, in a state of mental exhaustion, that it became clear.

"This probably won't make any sense," Tessa said. "But every time I felt Skylar's presence, I got the feeling that it was...draining him somehow. Like it took a lot of effort for him to be here."

Shannon bolted up, her face wild and alive. "Stay put," she said, then bounded up the stairs to her bedroom. Moments later, she returned carrying one of the books she'd read. She swiped through the pages until she located a certain passage.

"Listen to this," Shannon said. *"Afterlife researchers believe our deceased loved ones exist on a spiritual plane that operates on a different vibratory frequency than our own. In order for them to access the physical world, these spirits must lower their vibratory rate, which requires a tremendous amount of energy. It is for this reason that after-death communication often feels quick and incomplete."*

There was a burst of excitement between them. "What if," Shannon said, "he couldn't visit because he's—"

"Out of juice?" Tessa asked.

"Yes! Like he's only got one bar of battery left on his cell phone. So he has to go back to the bardo to recharge himself."

It all made sense now. Each ADC had been separated by a significant interval. Which likely meant that Skylar couldn't just come whenever he wanted. He had to conserve his energy and choose the perfect moment to cross the boundary between the here and the hereafter.

"We're just gonna have to try again," Shannon said. "When he's got a full charge."

Tessa felt a stab of panic. "Shan, there're only four days left before he's gone forever."

"Hey. He'll find a way. Skylar doesn't like to let go of things, remember?"

Of course she remembered. It was one of the most endearing—and annoying—things about Skylar. When he made a decision to accomplish something, he refused to give up, even when it meant convincing an insecure girl that she had talent.

Ping!

It was Tessa's cell phone. A text message from Vickie.

"Shit," Tessa said, realizing how late it was. "I forgot, Vickie's working the night shift. I've got to get her car back, stat."

Tessa pulled into her driveway and shut the engine. She glanced up to the second floor and saw Vickie peeking out her bedroom window, looking uncharacteristically peeved. Vickie had a deep well of patience for Tessa's mood swings and adolescent antics. But lateness, especially when it involved her work, was a third rail. She took her job at the casino seriously, and her pay would get docked if she was late. Tessa's only hope was that Vickie was in such a rush that she wouldn't have time to read her the riot act.

Tessa stepped onto the pavement and slammed the SUV's

door behind her. She walked up the brick pathway to the front door, but as her hand grasped the doorknob, she heard something behind her. It sounded like a voice.

She spun around, assuming it was a neighbor calling out to her. But there was no one there. The street before her was silent and eerily desolate.

"Hello?" Tessa said. "Is somebody here?"

There it was again. A voice. Muffled and indecipherable. It seemed to be repeating a few words on loop, like a record skipping on the same lyric. Tessa turned back down the pathway, trying to locate the source of the voice...getting closer... then farther away...then closer again. Finally, she realized the voice was coming from inside Vickie's car.

Maybe she'd left the stereo on? But how could the stereo be playing music when the car was off?

As Tessa edged closer to the SUV, she noticed the front seats were bathed in pale light. She pulled the key fob from her pocket and pressed the button. The alarm chirped and the locks popped up. Tessa pulled the door open and was met by a perfectly clear voice—the car's GPS. Its clinical, computer-generated intonation was repeating the same thing over and over again:

"*The route is being calculated....*"

"*The route is being calculated....*"

It didn't make sense. How could the GPS be working when the car wasn't even on? Tessa slipped into the driver's seat and studied the glowing GPS monitor. On it, she saw a map of her neighborhood. A tiny automobile icon indicated her current position. Suddenly, the screen blinked and a large arrow appeared on it.

"Please follow the route...."

"Please follow the route...."

Could it be him? Could Skylar be directing her somewhere?

"Please follow the route...."

"Please follow the route...."

Tessa saw the front door open. Through the screen door, she could see Vickie in the foyer, pulling her jacket on.

Tessa knew it was a mistake. She knew there'd be hell to pay, but she pressed the ignition button anyway. As Vickie stepped through the front door, Tessa punched the gear into *Reverse* and jammed her foot down on the gas pedal. The tires squealed and kicked up smoke as the car bolted out of the driveway.

At first, Vickie appeared stunned. But when she saw Tessa accelerating down the street, she took off after her. "Tessa! Where are you going?"

In the rearview, Tessa could see the distance between her and the house widen. Vickie finally stopped running, throwing her arms up in exasperation. Tessa felt a pang of guilt. Skylar had been right. Vickie deserved better.

When Tessa neared the stop sign at the end of her street, the GPS spoke again.

"Turn right on Douglas Avenue.... Please turn right...."

Tessa complied, turning the steering wheel, watching her

car's headlights sweep across the pavement. Up ahead, she saw Skylar's grandfather's house, its sprinklers sprouting umbrellas of water on the front lawn. Could this be her final destination, the place Skylar was taking her to ... ?

Evidently not. The GPS remained silent as Tessa cruised past the house, continuing up Douglas Avenue.

She was startled by the sound of ringing. It was her phone, which had paired itself to the SUV's Bluetooth. On the screen, Tessa noticed the street map had been replaced by the word *Vickie*. Tessa hit *Ignore*, then powered off her phone so there'd be no more interruptions.

She turned onto Ventnor Avenue. Up ahead, she saw a never-ending row of traffic lights that dangled over the street, changing in unison from green to yellow to red. The GPS spoke again, its voice expressionless: *"Please follow the road for three miles...."*

Three miles? Tessa glanced at the screen and saw an arrow pointing her onward, toward downtown Atlantic City. Hell, if that was where Skylar wanted her to go, then that was where she was going.

For the next twenty minutes, Tessa followed the GPS's prompts, zigzagging past dilapidated storefronts on ever-darkening streets. As she drove deeper into the city, she saw clusters of young men crowded in front of all-night bodegas, drinking alcohol from paper bags, eyeing Tessa as she cruised by. She was not in the safest neighborhood, and her heartbeat increased accordingly. Thankfully, she felt no pain. It seemed that her heart could finally handle a little stress.

She turned onto a residential street, lined on both sides with row homes. A few of them were already adorned with Halloween decorations, but for the most part, each one appeared indistinguishable from the next.

"You have reached your destination."

Tessa parked in front of a featureless residence. Through the living room window, she could see two people on a sofa, their faces pulsing with bluish light from a television set.

Could this be right? Why would Skylar direct her to a house she'd never seen, filled with people she didn't know? What did he expect her to do? Ring the doorbell and say, *Hey there! Sorry to bug you, but my dead boyfriend's spirit told me to come here!*

The thought made Tessa's heart beat even faster. But something inside nudged her to keep going. If she didn't knock on that door, she'd always wonder what would have happened. And regret was far worse than embarrassment.

Tessa stepped out of the car and onto the concrete path that led to the front door. She only made it a few steps when it happened. A searing, unbearable stab of pain in the center of her chest. Like a white-hot blade plunging through muscle and cartilage, over and over again. It was the most painful thing she'd ever experienced, an eleven on a scale of one to ten.

She tried taking deep breaths, but her lungs refused to fill with air. The world around her was spinning, her senses overwhelmed. Tessa staggered forward and threw her arms around the trunk of an old tree. She embraced the cold bark, straining to hold herself up. She knew she needed to focus on something other than the pain . . . something that would calm her heart. . . .

She thought of Skylar. He was on his lifeguard stand, shirtless, a silver whistle dangling around his tanned neck. Sometimes, on her days off, Tessa would visit his beach and spy on Skylar from afar. It was her little secret. She never told him or anyone else. She'd watch him charge into the ocean to save little kids or chat with pretty girls who were fruitlessly flirting with him. And all the while, Tessa would think: *He's mine.* On those days, Tessa didn't even need to talk to Skylar. Just knowing that he existed was enough for her.

The beautiful summer memories settled her heart. Her breathing became controlled and steady again. The pain abated.

Tessa gathered herself, wiping sweat from her forehead with the back of her sleeve. For a split second, she considered dialing 911, just as Dr. Nagash had instructed her. But she'd come this far. If she died in pursuit of Skylar, so be it.

She resumed her walk up the path. Her legs felt rigid and it took effort to move them. She pressed the doorbell but didn't hear anything ring inside the house. She tried it again. Still nothing. So she made a fist and knocked. A few seconds later, the door swung open.

A little boy, maybe ten years old, stood in the doorway. He had short-clipped hair and sweet, amber-colored eyes. He was dressed in a pair of pajamas that appeared two sizes too small for him.

Tessa forced a smile. "Hi. Uh. Sorry to bother you. My name's—"

"Come in, Tessa," said the boy. "We've been expecting you."

Huh? She'd never laid eyes on this kid before. He was a complete stranger. And yet, somehow, he knew her name and that she was coming to visit?

She followed the boy through the foyer and past the living room. There were three adults in there, two of them on the sofa, the third lying on the floor with his neck propped on a pillow. They were all watching a Spanish TV show. Only the man on the floor acknowledged Tessa's presence with a wave.

Tessa continued down the hall, trailing the boy past walls of framed photos. Faces of all ages stared out at her, but none looked familiar. Reaching the end of the hallway, the boy knocked lightly on a closed door, then turned to Tessa.

"*Mi abuela* keeps hearing a voice," the boy said. "The voice said he would bring you here."

He pushed the door open and Tessa stepped into the bedroom. It was stuffy and dark inside, lit solely by Santeria prayer candles. Tessa's gaze found the bed. On it, she saw a woman lying beneath layers of blankets, eyes closed, her face covered with an oxygen mask.

It was Doris.

She was on the precipice of death, connected to this world by a single remaining thread that was threatening to fray at any moment.

Tessa spoke quietly to the boy. "May I talk to her?"

"The medicine makes her sleepy," he said. "But you can try." The boy exited the room and shut the door behind him.

Tessa walked to the bedside. As if sensing a presence, Doris opened her eyes. She slid the oxygen mask from her face and smiled. "I told you he wasn't gone."

Tears began spilling from Tessa's eyes. If there were any doubts left, they were now gone. Skylar *was* reaching out to her.

Doris began to cough. It was a deep hack of mucus and fluids that gurgled inside her throat. Tessa grabbed a bottle of water from the nightstand and lifted the straw to Doris's lips. Doris swallowed some liquid and her throat settled.

"Is Skylar here? Now?" Tessa asked.

Doris nodded. Tessa eagerly looked around the room but saw nothing that resembled a ghost or apparition.

"I'm much closer to his world than you are. That's why I can sense him when you cannot," Doris said.

"What does he want?" Tessa asked.

"My help," Doris replied. "To bring the two of you together."

"Doesn't he know how?" Tessa asked.

"Skylar knows as much—and as little—as you do."

"Then how can we see each other? If he's there and I'm . . . here?"

Doris appeared focused now. "In ancient folklore, the souls of the deceased often returned to the places where they experienced the most love. It was there that they'd be able to cross the life-death barrier. Love was the key that opened the door. Perhaps if you and Skylar went back to the places where you felt closest, the portal between your worlds might open?"

With resolve, Tessa lifted her eyes from Doris and looked up to the ceiling. "I'll get to you, Skylar. No matter what it takes, I'll find a way."

Tessa pushed the oxygen mask back onto Doris's face, then stroked her hair tenderly. "There's nothing to be afraid of, Doris. Everyone you've ever lost will be waiting for you in the tunnel of light. It's the most beautiful place you've ever seen."

There was a blissful expression on Doris's face. "Yes. I know."

Mel was waiting up for her. The moment Tessa stepped into the house, she saw him alone in the living room, arms crossed. He was not pleased.

"Did Vickie make it to work okay?" Tessa asked.

"No thanks to you," Mel said sharply.

"Look, Mel, I'm sorry about tonight. I just—"

He cut her off. "You ever wonder why Vickie's working so much lately? Why she's doing doubles and the graveyard shift?"

Tessa shook her head. "I just figured—"

"It's because she's helping me pay off your medical bills."

Tessa flushed with guilt. She had no idea. She'd been so consumed by her own grief and the escalating series of supernatural events that she'd lost sight of what was going on with the people around her.

"Tess, I know you've been through a lot. No one knows more than I do how many bad breaks you've had. But if you're just gonna go back to the girl you were before you met Skylar, then what was the point of the summer? What was the point of falling in love?"

Mel rose to his feet. He walked past Tessa, up the stairs, and slammed his bedroom door shut. The vibration caused a framed photo to pop off the wall and shatter on the hardwood floor.

She kneeled down to pick up the frame. It was Mel and Vickie's wedding photo. Only now, there was a jagged crack running through their smiles.

thirty-
one
days
before

It was Skylar's fault she was underdressed. He never told her they were going to a gallery opening, so Tessa dressed casually, in a mini dress and old ballet flats. It was only when Skylar was parking his jeep in downtown Atlantic City that Tessa noticed he was wearing a sport jacket.

"Hang on," Tessa said. "Are we going somewhere fancy?"

Skylar cut the engine. "Just chill—you look fine."

"Fine?"

"Hot. Totally, undeniably hot."

They walked hand in hand down the sidewalk. It was a sketchy neighborhood, with one vacant shop after another, the street littered with crushed beer cans and fast-food wrappers. Up ahead, Tessa spotted a group of hipster types sharing a cigarette while sipping wine. They were standing by a store-front whose windows had been painted a hellish red, preventing anyone curious from seeing inside. A sign hanging over the door read PROJECT 82—ENTRANCE AROUND BACK.

Before they even turned into the alley, Tessa could hear the gentle pulse of electronic music and the din of a festive crowd. At the end of the alley, a pretty woman in a black jumpsuit stood behind a velvet rope, defending the gallery's entrance like a soldier. Skylar stopped before the woman and, mocking her self-importance, flashed a dopey smile.

"Hiya! I'm Skylar Adams. Linda put me on the list?"

Without making eye contact, the woman in black scanned her clipboard and crossed out Skylar's name with a pen. Then she unhooked the velvet rope and stepped back so Tessa and Skylar could enter. Her eyes never met theirs.

Inside, Tessa was met by whiteness. White walls, white ceilings, white floors. Everything was gleaming, including the crowd. Each guest was more beautiful than the next. And every one of them was dressed for the occasion. The men were in tailored suits and leather loafers, the women in designer dresses and terrifyingly high stilettos.

Tessa turned to Skylar. "Even the *caterers* are dressed better than we are."

"Sorry. I guess I wasn't thinking," Skylar said. He pointed to the exit. "Let's go. I don't want you to feel uncomfortable."

But strangely, Tessa did not feel the urge to retreat. She

guessed it had something to do with Skylar. Something about his presence always made her feel more confident, more beautiful.

"Let's just stay," Tessa said. "I want to see the art."

A few minutes later, holding plates of hors d'oeuvres, they stood before an enormous photo of a baby carriage teetering on the ledge of a cliff. Skylar leaned in, closer than he should have, to examine the image. Tessa yanked him back. "You're supposed to *look* at it, Sky, not drool on it."

"There's *so* much detail," he said.

"I think the artist coats his photos with barium sulfate. It soaks up the fiber of the paper and gives the image a greater tonal range."

"Exactly what I was gonna say."

"You want to buy it for me?" Tessa asked. "It's only twenty grand."

"Currently not in my budget. I can, however, offer you a gluten-free cracker with stinky cheese on top." He raised his plate and hovered it beneath her nose.

Amused, Tessa tilted her chin up, prompting Skylar to kiss her sweetly. She felt a familiar swell of excitement. Since the lake, she and Skylar had made good use of their time together. Almost every night, after work, they'd scramble to find a quiet place to make love. Sometimes, it was her darkroom. Other times, Skylar's bedroom while his grandfather slept in the neighboring room. One night, with nowhere else to go, they rented a cheap motel room near the ocean. Inside, with the curtains billowing from a summer breeze, they spent hours exploring each other.

There were several times, when their bodies were stitched together, that Tessa felt the words *I love you* straining to come out. But something continued to hold her back. It was as if she were at war with herself—part of her wanting to immerse herself fully in the relationship, the other part standing with her back pressed against a door, petrified of the beast pounding on the other side. More than anything, Tessa worried her silence was hurting Skylar's feelings. Despite his jock-ish exterior, she knew he was sensitive. Would Skylar, the hopeless romantic, tolerate an entire summer without hearing the words back? For now, he'd chosen not to bring it up again. But how long would that last?

"Pardon me, am I interrupting...?"

Standing behind them was an attractive woman in her early forties. She was in a spaghetti-strap black dress, and it was obvious she'd spent hours at the gym working to sculpt her arms into showstoppers.

"Hey, Linda, good to see you," Skylar said.

The woman gave Skylar a friendly kiss on his cheek, which left a faint trace of her lipstick on his face. She gestured to the print on the wall with admiration. "It's wonderful, isn't it?"

"I love the way the artist prioritizes mood and atmosphere over subject," Tessa said.

Linda seemed pleasantly surprised by Tessa's observation. "Well, well. That's a *very* sophisticated insight for a girl your age."

"Linda," Skylar said. "Meet my very sophisticated girlfriend—"

"Who has a name." Tessa held out her hand. "Tessa Jacobs. Nice to meet you."

"Linda's the one who put me on the list. This is her gallery."

"Congratulations," Tessa said brightly. "The photographs are wonderful."

Linda grinned with pride. "What else can a forty-four-year-old woman do with her divorce settlement? Beach house? Got one. New boobs? Been there, done that. But an art gallery . . . now *that's* something that can bring you into the orbit of rich, single men." She winked at Tessa, seeking approval. Unsure of how to respond, Tessa winked back.

"So, Tessa, did your boyfriend tell you I'm forever in his debt? He saved my daughter's life."

Tessa turned to Skylar. "So *that's* how you scored an invite to this gala?"

"Perks of the day job," Skylar said with a smirk.

"It was like a scene from *Baywatch*," Linda said. "Skylar swam out through the crashing waves and scooped my little angel into his arms. He even gave her mouth-to-mouth! Oh, look, there's Bobbi now."

Tessa gazed through the crowd and spotted Bobbi, who appeared to be around her same age. Like her mother, Bobbi was tall and slim, with perfectly tanned skin that glistened under the gallery lights. But it was her lips that were impossible to ignore. They were big, swollen, and naturally inflated—the kind that were irresistibly kissable.

Holy crap! Skylar gave this runway model mouth-to-mouth?

When Bobbi noticed her mother waving, her eyes lit up, and she flashed a dazzling smile. She walked through the crowd like a movie star, towering over everyone in her four-inch pumps. She swept past Tessa and eagerly threw her arms around Skylar. She kissed him in the same spot her mother had, placing a much-larger lipstick stain on his face.

"I'm *so* happy you made it!" Bobbi said.

Clearly anticipating Tessa's discomfort, Skylar disentangled himself from Bobbi's embrace. He swung his arm around Tessa's back, squeezing her reassuringly. "Bobbi, I want you to meet my girlfriend, Tessa."

"Hey, you!" Bobbi said brightly.

After they shook hands, Tessa felt a trace of Bobbi's lotion on her palm. It was radiating a tropical scent. Bobbi quickly turned her attention back to Skylar. "Daddy asked for your address, Skylar. He wants to send you something as a thank-you."

"That's not necessary. It's my job, I get paid to do it."

"Oh, stop," Linda said. "You saved a human life—you should accept the gift. Trust me, he was a shitty hubby but an amazing gift giver."

How delightful, Tessa thought. *It's a family affair now.* Mommy absolutely adored Skylar, Daddy wanted to send him swag, and little Bobbi was gazing dreamily at him, jonesing to lay those duck lips on him.

"So? Are you ready for the big reveal?" Linda asked Tessa.

"Big reveal?"

"He didn't tell you?"

"There's a lot Skylar didn't tell me about tonight," Tessa quipped.

"Including what to wear," Bobbi said, flashing a patronizing smile.

Led by Linda, the four of them walked through the crowd, a river of exquisite faces flowing past Tessa on both sides. Turning the corner, they entered another part of the gallery, where the smaller works of art were on display. They arrived before a framed black-and-white photo, hung at eye level. It was lit by a tiny spotlight. It took Tessa a few seconds to comprehend what she was looking at. . . . *It was her photo*, the one of the cell-phone tower. It had been expertly matted and framed in museum-quality wood. Beneath the photo, written on a small rectangle, was Tessa's full name (TESSA JACOBS) along with her country of origin (UNITED STATES).

"Doesn't it look awesome framed up?" Skylar said with excitement. "Like it belongs here."

"It *does* belong here," Linda replied. "You've got an extraordinary eye, Tessa. I see great things in your future."

"I don't . . . understand?" Tessa mumbled.

"It's for sale!" Skylar said. "For five hundred dollars!"

"And here's the best part," Linda added. "I've already received two serious inquiries tonight."

"Congratulations," said Bobbi, her eyes still glued to Skylar.

The betrayal cut deep. How could Skylar think this was okay? She'd given him the photo as a gift, as an expression of her desire to open herself up to him. She could have never guessed that he would just give it away without even asking her. Did he not understand her at all? What was the point of telling him everything about her past if he wasn't going to understand her vulnerabilities?

"I'm sorry, Linda," Tessa said. "But there's been a mistake.... This photo—*my* photo—it's not for sale. It was a gift. To Skylar."

"Why can't you just print me another?" Skylar asked.

"Because," Tessa said, "I don't want anyone looking at it." She turned back to Linda. "Could you take it down? *Please?*"

There was an air of discomfort now. Mystified, Bobbi turned to Skylar. "Is she being serious right now?"

"Yes, I'm being serious! Take it down!" Tessa screamed. "Take it down now!"

The tone of her voice silenced the noisy chatter. People were staring at Tessa. They were probably wondering who that psycho girl was—the one dressed for a barbecue—and why she was making a scene.

Embarrassed, Tessa shoved Skylar out of her way and pushed through the crowd, clearing a path to the exit. Emerging from the side alley, she began running, trying to get away . . . away from the gallery and Skylar and the girl with the cartoon lips who smelled like Hawaii.

Now on the sidewalk, Tessa heard Skylar calling to her. "Tessa! Wait up!"

Out of breath, Tessa spun around to face him. She was furious. "How could you do that?"

"You mean try and help you?"

"You—of all people—know how insecure I am about my work!"

"That's exactly why I brought you here! To prove to you that there's nothing to be insecure about. Your photos are great. Even Linda thinks so."

"Oh, come on, *of course* she's gonna say that! You saved her daughter's life."

"I only asked Linda for an opinion. *She* was the one who offered to sell it."

"Skylar, I gave that photo to *you* and *only you*. I don't want it hanging on the wall of some rando stranger."

"News flash: Being an artist means sharing your work with others. You think Picasso met everyone who bought one of his paintings?"

Tessa felt blood rising to her face. "I'm *not* Picasso! And I don't like it when you talk down to me like that. It's *my* photo, which means *I* get to decide who I share it with!"

She saw something shift in Skylar's eyes. It was as if her anger had wilted a blooming flower inside him. Until that moment, he hadn't realized he'd done something wrong. Somehow, in trying to help her, he'd done the opposite.

"I'm really sorry," Skylar said, his voice laced with regret. "You're right. I should have asked you first. I just . . . I dunno . . . I figured you'd be excited. Most people would be."

"I'm not most people."

"Yeah, I'm beginning to figure that out," he said.

His words stung her. So she stung back. "You can't fix everything, Sky."

"What's that supposed to mean?"

"Your parents' marriage...me. Sometimes things are broken and can't be fixed."

Skylar's face hardened. "Is that why you won't tell me you love me? Because you can't be fixed?"

What had remained unmentioned since the lake was now out in the open.

"You know something, Tessa? You always say you're not ready to share your work with the world. But maybe you're not ready to share *yourself.*"

On the drive back, they did not exchange a single word. When Skylar pulled to a stop outside Tessa's house, he didn't shut his engine, and his eyes remained forward. There was a pit of anger and anxiety gnawing inside Tessa. She felt like she wanted to explode. To scream, to cry, to tell him how scared she was—scared for their future, scared she wasn't good enough for him, and most of all, scared of revealing how much she loved him. But Tessa said none of these things.

Instead, she climbed out of the jeep and walked up the brick pathway. At the door, like always, she spun around to signal to Skylar that she was okay.

But his jeep was already gone.

twenty-
two
days
before

FOR HER LUNCH BREAK, TESSA SAT AT HER USUAL BENCH ON THE Boardwalk. It was a humid August day, and splotches of sweat were forming beneath her T-shirt. In front of her, she watched couples, families, and children playing on the beach, enjoying the final weeks of summer. All of them seemed happy. Tessa used to think happiness was a myth, an elaborate performance that people played for the purpose of making others jealous. But this summer, Tessa's attitude had changed. She *was* happy. Skylar made her happy. And now that happiness had been torn away.

The pit inside her stomach, the one that had opened the night of their argument, was making it difficult for her to concentrate on anything. She wasn't hungry, but she forced herself to take a few bites of the tuna sandwich Vickie had packed for her.

Since their first date, Tessa and Skylar had been in constant communication—calls, texts, emails. Even on the rare days they didn't see each other, they'd end their nights chatting on FaceTime. But now, after their argument at the gallery, radio silence.

It pissed Tessa off. Why wasn't he calling? *He* was the one who had messed up. Granted, he'd apologized, but Tessa still felt like he needed to acknowledge how presumptuous he'd been with her photo. He needed to be the one who called first, because...because...

Was it pride? Or something deeper? Something Tessa was afraid to admit? That maybe—just maybe—there was a part of her that was looking for a way out? After all, with their relationship over, she'd never have to say *I love you* to him.

After her lunch break, Tessa decided to text Skylar. She typed out a few different messages but eventually settled on a single word, *hey*, followed by a sad emoji face. She hoped the text would elicit a friendly response from him. But by the time her workday ended, he still had not replied. And for the first time since their fight, Tessa felt intensely frightened. Had she underestimated how upset he was? She'd never been in a serious relationship before. She had nothing to compare this to. Was this what breaking up looked like?

On the bus ride home, Tessa felt her phone vibrate in her pocket. Her heart surged. Maybe Skylar had texted her back? Nope. It was just Mel, reminding her to pick up dinner on her way home that night. Great, here she was, sifting through the ruins of her first relationship, and all Mel could do was remind her to order extra cheese on his meatball pizza.

Tessa remembered that she and Skylar had talked about going to the Little Art Theater that Saturday night. Sherman was playing a spaghetti western double feature, and Skylar had mentioned he wanted to go. That felt like a good excuse to reach out again. She typed another text.

TESSA: Are we still on for the movies tomorrow night?

She pressed *Send* and waited, staring at the screen....

She waited some more....

Just as she was about to stuff her phone away, Tessa noticed three dots flashing on her screen, indicating that Skylar was typing a response. She felt a rush of relief. She could finally get this damn weight off her back. They could resume their relationship as if nothing had happened. No, actually, they'd be closer now because they'd successfully navigated their first big fight.

Her phone vibrated in her palm.

SKYLAR: I need to cancel.

Her stomach dropped. He was still mad. So mad that he didn't even want to see her.

TESSA: How come?

More dots. More waiting...

SKYLAR: My father showed up in Princeton unannounced. It got super messy.

Okay, so it *wasn't* about her. That was a relief. But then, if it wasn't about their fight, why was Skylar being so cold? He was treating her like a stranger.

TESSA: Ouch. I'm really sorry.

More dots. More waiting...

SKYLAR: I'm driving up tonight to see what I can do. I'll call you when I'm back.

What more could Tessa say? How could she tell him that she wanted to make things right? She typed out three words.

TESSA: I miss you.

Her thumb hovered over the *Send* icon. But for some reason, she couldn't find the nerve to press it. Pride had gotten the better of her.

twenty-
one
days
before

"Okay," Vickie said. "It's eight o'clock, I'm here like you asked. What's up?"

Tessa was sitting on a stool, clutching her camera, which she'd just loaded with film. For a split second, Tessa felt her usual knee-jerk irritation at seeing Vickie in her space. But tonight, Tessa couldn't say anything snarky, as she'd personally extended the invitation. She needed advice. *Adult* advice. From a woman, not a girl. Thus, the invitation.

Vickie was dressed in loose-fitting sweats, her hair held up by a fluorescent scrunchie. She looked exhausted, her eyes sunken. As a blackjack dealer at one of the local casinos, Vickie was on her feet for eight-hour shifts, sometimes two shifts back-to-back. By the time she returned home, she was an exhausted lump of flesh that reeked of stale cigar smoke.

Tessa rose from the stool. Behind her, she had created a makeshift backdrop by draping a white sheet across her dark-room wall. Tessa flipped a switch, and a half dozen pre-arranged lights blinked on simultaneously, like a Christmas tree coming to life.

"I'd like to take your portrait," Tessa said.

Vickie was puzzled at first. Was this some kind of practical joke? But then, when she saw the seriousness in Tessa's expression, tears brimmed in her eyes, indicating that Vickie understood the meaning of Tessa's olive branch.

Vickie and Tessa had lived under the same roof for a year and a half, but in all that time, Tessa had not taken a single photo of Vickie. Not on Christmas morning, not on the camping trip they took to Vermont, not even when Vickie won Dealer of the Year at work. By not pointing her camera at Vickie, Tessa was sending the message that Vickie was insignificant—and just like all the others, not worthy of Tessa's viewfinder.

But as the summer unfolded, something about the way she'd been treating Vickie began to bother Tessa. Of all the people in her life, why was Tessa meanest to the woman who'd been nothing but generous to her? Naturally, it was Skylar who helped Tessa stumble on the answer when he said, "You're right—Vickie's not your mom. She loves you way more than your mom ever did."

Was it possible that Tessa had been directing her rage at the wrong target? Wasn't it her real mother—the one who'd discarded her like trash—who deserved Tessa's reproach? It was as if Tessa had once been attacked by a ferocious pit bull—and now, years later, any dog that came near her, even a cute puppy, was a mortal enemy.

"Is it okay if I change first?" Vickie asked.

"Just put this on," Tessa said, lifting a garment from a hook.

Vickie unfurled the jumble of fabric. She looked surprised to discover it was a white dress, made of thin muslin. Its texture was similar to gauze. "Is it...see-through?" she asked.

"Chill," Tessa said. "You've got the body to pull it off."

Vickie smiled, a mutinous expression on her face. "Oh, fuck it."

Minutes later, Vickie was sitting on the stool, the dress clinging to the curves of her body. After Tessa adjusted the lighting, Vickie was bathed in a web of shadow and light, only the faintest hint of her body visible to the naked eye.

Tessa began to take photos, but Vickie appeared tense, her poses deliberate and stiff. Tessa tried coaching her but had no experience taking portraits. Eventually, she decided that music might loosen things up. She switched on her Spotify app and cranked up Vickie's favorite playlist, a collection of '90s songs by female singers like Sarah McLachlan and Alanis Morissette. Tessa jokingly referred to the playlist as "estrogen music."

Almost immediately, Vickie's poses became looser and more natural. At one point, lost in the moment, Vickie liberated her ponytail from the scrunchie and shook her hair out like a supermodel. She shouted above the music, "This brings me back!"

"Back to when?" Tessa asked.

"College. University of Wisconsin. My boyfriend Dale was an art major. He was seriously hot. Like, Brad Pitt hot. A bunch of times, he asked me to undress and pose for him."

Fascinated, Tessa lowered her camera. "You let him paint you...naked?"

"I was a lot younger then," Vickie said pridefully. "My boobs were like missiles, you should have seen them. They were perky as hell."

Tessa couldn't believe it. She was seeing a side of Vickie that she never imagined was there. Adventurous, cocky, even brave.

"So...Mel's not the first person you've been in love with?" Tessa asked.

Vickie chuckled. "God no. I've loved a whole bunch of guys. And maybe even one woman. But don't you dare tell that to Mel."

Tessa nodded, indicating Vickie's secret was safe. "Did you love any of those guys more than they loved you?"

"I'm sure I did."

"Didn't that scare you? Knowing they could hurt you more than you could hurt them?"

"At first, yes. But then I realized if I tried to protect myself from the lows, I'd only wind up protecting myself from the highs. In which case, why even go through with it?"

Tessa went silent. It had never occurred to her that hold-ing back wasn't just hurting Skylar but hurting her, too. How much more joy could she glean from their relationship if she opened her heart completely?

"You love Skylar, don't you?" Vickie asked.

Tessa nodded reluctantly. "And I'm totally screwing it up."

"I'm sure you're exaggerating."

"It's like this reflex. Every time we get closer, this scared little girl inside me comes out and pushes him away."

"Have you told him what you've been through? As a child?"

"Yes. And he's been totally accepting of it. He told me he loves me. But I don't know how to stop pushing him away. I don't know how to make him understand that I love him."

"Well, you can start by saying it."

Tessa sighed bleakly. "Why did I know you were going to say that?"

"You need to hear the words, Tessa."

"You mean *he* needs to hear the words."

"No, Tessa. *You* need to hear yourself saying those words. Out loud. When you use those three words, you're telling yourself that your feelings count. That *you* count. You're tell-ing the world that you're not going to let that scared little girl inside silence your heart."

Vickie was now standing across from Tessa. And for the first time ever, Tessa allowed Vickie to hug her. The warmth and love Tessa felt in that moment unleashed a torrent of pent-up shame.

"I'm so sorry for how I've treated you, Vickie," Tessa said through sobs.

"I know you are, Tess."

And just like that, in an attic darkroom, at half past ten on a warm August night, Vickie became Tessa's mom.

sixteen
days
before

WHEN MR. DUFFY OPENED HIS FRONT DOOR, TESSA BURST OUT laughing. She'd never seen him wear anything other than a collared shirt and paisley tie. But here he was, standing in his doorway, barefoot, dressed in a brown terry bathrobe. His blond hair, usually swept up impeccably, was matted down like pancake batter that had been dumped over his scalp.

"Tessa? What are you doing here?"

"Crap!" Tessa said. "Did I get the days mixed up?" But she was just being nice. Of course Tessa hadn't mixed up the days. It was Thursday morning at eight, the time they had agreed over email to meet.

"Jeez, I'm sorry, Tessa. I—uh—rarely check my calendar during the summer."

"Should I come back later?"

"No, no—you're here now, come on in."

It was a modest home, befitting a modest man. The old hardwood floors creaked beneath Tessa's feet as she followed him into his living room.

Mr. Duffy took the leather portfolio from Tessa's hands and gestured for her to sit on the sofa. He unzipped the portfolio and spread it across the coffee table. He sat down in a chair across from her.

"Okay," he said. "Let's see what you've got."

And then, with great care and thoughtfulness, Mr. Duffy began to page through Tessa's photos.

After her conversation with Vickie, Tessa knew she had to tell Skylar she loved him. But she didn't just want to *tell* him; she wanted to *show* him. And she decided the best way to do that would be to apply to RISD. Granted, the odds of her getting in were minuscule. Thousands applied every year and only a few hundred were accepted. But the mere fact that she had made the effort would send Skylar a message: Tessa wanted them to be together.

So she had reworked her portfolio, incorporating the best of her summer photos. Now, alongside the dreary landscapes and cell-phone towers, there were images of Skylar, his grandfather Mike, and Shannon and Judd. Tessa even added one of the risqué portraits she'd taken of Vickie the week before. In fact, it was among her favorite photographs now—a poignant reminder of the mother-daughter bond they'd forged in the darkroom.

As Mr. Duffy paged through the portfolio, Tessa saw a myriad of emotions appear on his face. But mostly, she saw pride.

"It's unbelievable," Mr. Duffy declared with excitement. "It's like you've discovered a completely different muscle. So many faces, so many *people*."

"So you think I have a chance?"

"Absolutely. I'm certain the admissions board will be impressed."

"They better be. Without a scholarship, there's no way I can afford to go."

"I'll be sure to mention your financial situation to my friend on the admissions board. In the meantime, you're still going to have to present your work at their portfolio day in November."

"Do I have to?" Tessa said hesitantly. Mr. Duffy knew better than anyone that Tessa hated public speaking. She got nervous standing before a classroom of twenty kids. How was she going to present her work to an auditorium filled with hundreds of talented photographers her own age, not to mention the entire admissions committee?

"One step at a time, Tessa," Mr. Duffy said reassuringly.

"I guess I can always practice in the mirror?"

"Yes. Then, when you feel comfortable, ask your parents to be your audience."

Your parents.

Normally, Tessa would snap at anyone using those words. But today, she liked how they sounded.

"Tell me, Tessa.... What changed your mind? Last school

year, you were *so* adamant about not going to college. You claimed you didn't have the talent to get in."

Tessa flashed a mischievous smile. "Remember when you told me what Sally Mann said? That in order to find your voice, you need to find someone to love?"

"I remember."

"Well," she said with a twinkle in her eye. "I did."

thirty-
seven
days
after

THREE DAYS LEFT.

A plan began to form in Tessa's mind. It was a plan born of both necessity and time. Tessa only had three days to locate the portal to the bardo. If she could not reach Skylar by then, she never would.

First things first. She needed to create a list of all the places where she and Skylar had experienced something significant together. Despite the fact that they'd only been dating for a few months, this was not as easy as it seemed. They'd crammed a lot of experiences into that time. And looking back, even inconsequential moments held meaning. There was that time in the drugstore, when Skylar dared Tessa to shoplift a box of candy bars and she got caught by the manager. There was also their epic watermelon fight, the one that left them both drenched in bright red juice. How could you calculate love? How could you determine which event, which moment, which glance or smile or kiss had the most significance? It was impossible. And that was why Tessa's first list was seven pages long and had 273 possible locations, far too many for her to visit in three days. She needed to cut the list down.

She kept at it, reducing seven pages to two, which left her with thirty-two places, still too many to reasonably visit in seventy-two hours. Tessa tried once more, this time delving into the deepest recesses of her heart in order to determine which moments meant the most to her—and which moments likely meant the most to Skylar. After much hand-wringing, she whittled the list down to three places:

1. *The Little Art Theater (where we first met).*
2. *The Empyrean Hotel (where we first kissed).*
3. *The lake (where Skylar told me he loved me).*

Three locations. Three days. That was doable.

The next part of her plan required her to buy some specialized gear. Since Doris had told her that disembodied spirits could manipulate electricity, Tessa decided to break with her long-standing aversion to modern equipment and buy a digital camera. The new camera would serve two purposes. First, its battery would help provide Skylar's spirit with energy, thus lengthening the duration of their potential interaction. Second, the camera would have an advanced low-light setting.

This would help her capture Skylar's spirit in a photo, assuming he was able to materialize visually.

She needed to go see Sol.

Unlike other locally owned shops on Margate's main street, Sol's Photo Shop had not succumbed to rising rents and e-commerce. That was because its namesake, Sol, owned the building that housed his store. And Sol made enough money from renting the neighboring space that he could keep his decaying store afloat. Tessa had been Sol's best customer for two years, and they'd developed a friendly rapport. She was counting on that relationship when she entered his store and handed him a list of equipment whose cost exceeded two thousand dollars.

While waiting at the register, Tessa watched Sol through the stockroom door. He had identical tufts of gray hair sprouting from both sides of his head. They seemed to defy gravity and stood perpendicular to his face, like a clown's wig. As he rummaged through various shelves for Tessa's equipment, the tufts flapped up and down like wings. She heard him grousing to himself. He was frustrated, clearly unable to locate something amid the junkyard of inventory scattered around the stockroom.

"You okay?" Tessa called out.

Sol emerged from the back of the store, balancing a stack of cube-shaped boxes in his arms. He placed the boxes side by side on the countertop, then ticked off each piece of equipment while referring to Tessa's list. "Full-spectrum digital camera with night-vision capabilities...motion-activated infrared illumination. And last but not least, enough batteries to power a cruise ship."

Sol studied the merchandise on the counter below him and identified a theme. "Hell, if I didn't know any better, I'd say you were going ghost hunting."

Without answering, Tessa slapped a credit card onto the glass counter. "Just ring it up."

Sol picked up the card, but before he ran it through the reader, he clocked the name on it. *Shit. Here we go.*

"Does Mel know you're using his card?" Sol asked.

"Of course. It's my birthday present."

"Birthday present? It's October, your birthday's in April."

Tessa flashed a devilish smile. "Not this year."

Sol looked uneasy. So uneasy that Tessa worried he'd insist on calling Mel in order to get his approval. The last time Mel caught Tessa "borrowing" money from his wallet, he grounded her for two months and confiscated her phone. Borrowing his credit card was a much greater transgression.

"Is it all right if I call Mel, just to put my mind at ease?"

"You don't trust me, Sol?" Tessa asked.

"You remember what President Reagan said? *Trust but verify.*" Sol reached to pick up his old landline phone, but Tessa grabbed his wrist with urgency, stopping him.

"For fuck's sake, Sol, just ring it up."

Sol sighed like he knew something was fishy, but he didn't seem to have the courage to argue.

"Fine," he said. "But it's on your conscience, not mine."

She had no choice. She *had* to lie to Sherman. It didn't make her feel good, but would he—or anyone else—believe the truth? *Hey, Sherman, I need your movie theater all to myself tonight so I can open a doorway to the afterworld in order to reunite with my dead boyfriend.* So she told Sherman she was working on a project for art class. All she needed was a few hours alone to take some photos. The lie worked.

At eleven o'clock that night, Tessa found herself in the empty movie theater, unpacking her new equipment. She slipped a fully charged battery into her digital camera and clicked its tiny door shut. Next, she secured her new camera onto the mount of her tripod and clipped the motion-activated infrared light to one of its legs. This would activate the camera's shutter when it detected any kind of movement. Finally, Tessa placed the tripod one row down from the center of the theater, pointing her camera at the seats she and Skylar had once occupied. After wiping the lens free of smudges, Tessa sat in her original seat and took a deep, anxious breath.

What now? she thought. Without any kind of rule book, Tessa was flying blind. So she waited. In the musty theater. Alone. The movie screen before her was a rectangle of dimmed whiteness. Occasionally, she heard soft creaking noises that raised her hopes, but she realized it wasn't Skylar's ghost; it was wind blowing against the theater's exterior walls.

What, exactly, was Tessa expecting? For Skylar to sit down next to her? Was that even realistic? She felt a sudden jab of doubt. She began to consider what Doris had told her, how returning to the places she and Skylar felt closest might *open a portal*. But maybe being here, in this spot, wasn't enough? Maybe she needed to *do* something? No, she needed to *feel something*. Yes, that was it. It wasn't the *location* that was important; it was the *feelings* she'd experienced there. It was the joy she felt in these places that would call Skylar forth.

Tessa had once read about a technique that the greatest actors used. If they needed to feel sad, they'd scour their memories for a painful moment from their past. Then they'd marinate in that memory, encouraging the emotion to rise up like a buoy. Once the memory surfaced, they'd be able to perform the scene with stunning realism. It was called "sense memory." And that was what Tessa needed to do.

It wasn't difficult to commune with the past. Everything was still fresh in her mind. It had been eight months since they first met in the theater, but like a forceful undertow, the memories began to tug her back...back to the moment when Skylar first sat down next to her....

She could recall the woody scent that radiated off his body...his first words, *You watch, I'll translate*...the warmth of his breath on her neck...his green eyes when the lights faded up...their conversation about love stories and happy endings....

Tessa was tumbling through a maelstrom of nostalgia, sadness, and joy. She lost track of time. Was she here, in the now? Or back there, in the then? The line between past and present, between memory and physical reality, became indistinct.

"It's two in the morning, Tessa."

Sherman's voice snapped Tessa back. He was standing in the aisle, his eyelids heavy.

"Just a little while longer, Sherman?"

"Maybe tomorrow," he said regretfully.

There was no point in arguing. Tessa had already overstayed her welcome. And anyway, the first place on her list, the place where she had met Skylar, did not produce anything but desperate longing for him.

One down. Two to go.

thirty-
eight
days
after

TWO DAYS LEFT.

It was past seven when Tessa stepped into the Empyrean honeymoon suite. As far as she could tell, nothing had changed. The carpet was still soiled, the curtains were still faded and torn, and paint was still peeling off the walls in curled ribbons.

She unpacked her equipment next to the champagne Jacuzzi. Like the previous night in the theater, she fastened her camera to her tripod and clipped the infrared sensor to one of its legs. Then she rotated the camera, pointing its lens to the exact spot where Skylar had kissed her for the first time.

Satisfied that everything was in order, Tessa climbed up the ladder and lowered herself into the Jacuzzi. The tub's floor was littered with cigarette butts and empty glass bottles.

Evidently, others had discovered their secret little place, and it angered Tessa that they had not treated it with the reverence it deserved.

Tessa leaned back, reclining against the sloped wall of the champagne glass. After squeezing her wireless earbuds in, she opened the music app on her phone and pressed her thumb to the *Repeat* symbol. Then, after a short pause, their song, "More Than This," began to play....

The song's familiar chords achieved their intended purpose, instantly drawing Tessa back...back to the past...to before...before her world turned dark....

Consciousness dimmed. She felt as though she was standing on a high diving board, overlooking a pristine pool of crystal clear water. Suspended within that water was the memory of their first date. Eager to enter the past, Tessa spread her arms like wings and sprang off the board within her mind. She was momentarily aloft, a majestic bird in flight, before plunging into the pleasantly warm water.

Now she was inside her memory, indivisible from it. The sound of Skylar's laughter rippled through the water around her.... Tessa felt the same butterflies she'd felt that night in the hotel suite, her stomach whirling with anticipation.... And then his lips—his beautiful lips—pressing softly, then urgently, against hers.

Tessa began to feel a strange tickling sensation dancing over her body. Her attention detoured back to the song. Somehow, it had changed. It was no longer their song. Instead, she heard a strumming guitar and a sweet voice singing lyrics she'd never heard before. The song was quaint and heartfelt, something recorded in a more innocent time, the 1960s perhaps.

Tessa's eyes fluttered open. She must have fallen asleep in the Jacuzzi. She rubbed her eyes to clear them, but everything was hazy and rippling. She realized she was still underwater, which meant she was still dreaming.

No, if she were dreaming, she wouldn't feel the distinct, tight pinch of her wireless earbuds in her ears. There was a difference between dreaming and being awake, and this was awake. But why was she underwater? And how was she *breathing* underwater?

Frightened, Tessa bolted upward. She found herself still inside the Jacuzzi, only now it was filled with water up to her chest. She instinctively reached to brush her bangs away from her forehead but discovered her hair wasn't wet. Puzzled, she raked her fingers across the water's surface and was shocked to see it remain undisturbed.

It's not real water. It's something else. Like . . . the image of water being projected into the tub.

Gazing over the Jacuzzi's rim, Tessa saw the suite had changed. Somehow, all its furnishings were brand-new. The shag carpet that, minutes earlier, had been a mass of dirt and dust was now bright and clean. The two-post bed had four posts again, its mattress covered with clean linens. It was as if Tessa had stepped through a time machine and was now seeing the room in its original condition from the 1960s.

Beside the bed, Tessa noticed an enormous radio resting on the shelf of an oak credenza. It was this radio that was blasting the sweet song that had stirred her awake.

Equally baffled and intrigued, Tessa rose to her feet. She noticed that her clothes were bone-dry; not a single drop of water had fallen off her. She climbed over the rim of the Jacuzzi and down the ladder. When her foot touched the floor, Tessa was startled by a sudden, bright flash of light. She whirled around in shock. It was her camera. The motion detector had caught Tessa's movement and fired the flash and shutter. At least now she knew it worked.

Tessa began to walk through the room, taking in all the details that had once been disguised by age and neglect. Up above, the ceilings were covered with mirrors arranged in a starburst pattern. And the curtains—they weren't dark brown after all; they were the color of freshly cut roses. The decor's elegance was startling. It made Tessa think of the wedding photo that hung on Grandpa Mike's living room wall, the one of his young bride. *Time hides so much beauty*, she thought.

Tessa turned to the credenza that housed the radio. Wanting to lower the music to a reasonable level, she reached for the silvery volume knob, but her hand went straight through it, as if she weren't there. Was she a ghost? No, she was still solid and real. Maybe it was the other way around? Maybe everything in the room, everything she saw, was some kind of ghostly projection? Was that even possible? Tessa had always thought of ghosts as people. Could objects be intangible, too?

At that moment, Tessa felt a subtle shift in the room. *Flash!* Her camera shutter clicked on its own again. Something was moving behind her. She spun around and saw the air before her shimmering, like waves of heat radiating off hot asphalt. Her camera was going crazy now—*Flash! Flash! Flash!*—snapping pictures rapidly.

It felt as though all the atoms and particles that comprised the hotel room were communicating with one another and directing their energy to a single spot in front of Tessa's eyes. Suddenly, a tiny sphere of light, no larger than a baseball, appeared in midair. It was made of the same golden-white light that Tessa had seen when she was in the tunnel, rushing toward the afterworld. The sphere began oscillating, its circumference widening, like an iris was opening. A blast of warm light erupted through the opening, splashing across Tessa's face. She instinctively raised her hand to shield her eyes from the brightness but found it wasn't necessary. She could stare directly into it. Now, on the other side of the chasm, Tessa could see the contours of a human figure. It was a figure she'd studied as deeply as any photo she'd fallen in love with....

Skylar.

"Oh my God," Tessa said.

He was standing before her, half-solid, half-vaporous. His body was misty and indistinct, but his face was defined enough to make out his features. Upon seeing him for the first time since the accident, Tessa released a frantic cry of joy. Tears ran freely down her face. So overwhelmed by emotion, she could not form a single word. She could only marvel at his presence, wishing she could hold on to this euphoria forever.

Skylar waved his hand, motioning for Tessa to come closer. She willed her feet forward and arrived at the borderline of the chasm, now inches from his diaphanous face. In Skylar's expression, she saw longing. Their bodies were tantalizingly close, yet they were unbearably separate and apart.

Yearning to touch him, Tessa reached out. But when her hand crossed the threshold, it evaporated, and she could not see or feel it anymore. Fearful, she quickly yanked her hand back.

It was Skylar's turn to try. He reached through the chasm, and as his hand passed the dividing line, it, too, disappeared. But moments later, Tessa felt Skylar's invisible touch, gliding down her face, wiping her tears away. She shuddered.

There was a pained look on Skylar's face. It was, she suspected, the first time he had touched human flesh since his soul had separated from his body.

"Sky? Can you hear me?"

Skylar shrugged in confusion. He did not appear to understand her words. His mouth moved, but Tessa couldn't hear him. Sound, it seemed, could not cross the barrier that separated them.

Suddenly, Skylar's expression changed. There was panic in his eyes. At that moment, the portal began shrinking. In desperation, he reached out to Tessa as though trying to grab on to her.

"Skylar, wait!" she cried out. "Come back!"

But the chasm closed with jarring finality, just as Tessa heard a deep voice call out to her. "Are you Tessa Jacobs?"

She turned. A tall, burly shadow of a man filled the suite's doorway. He was shining a flashlight into Tessa's eyes.

"Who are you?" Tessa asked, her voice breaking with fear. "What do you want?"

The flashlight blinked off, and Tessa saw a police officer standing before her.

"I'm Officer Rogers," he said. "Your parents are looking for you."

As the officer led her out of the suite, Tessa took one final look back. The room had returned to its dilapidated condition. And the Jacuzzi was just an empty tub of cigarette butts and cracked beer bottles.

It was as if nothing had ever happened.

Officer Rogers had left ten minutes earlier, but Tessa was still on her front lawn, screaming at Mel and Vickie.

"You put spyware on my phone! I can't even—"

Mel's face was red, his eyes slits of anger. "The moment you stole my credit card was the moment you gave up your right to privacy!"

Vickie was doing her best to stay calm, but Mel's anger was infectious, like a virus passing between them. "For God's sake, Tessa, what the hell were you doing at that hotel? Don't addicts and homeless people live there?"

"I told you, I was taking photos!"

"At this hour?" Vickie said. "On a school night?"

"She's *deliberately* trying to put herself back in the hospital!" Mel screamed.

Tessa didn't have time for this. "And what if I am? Being dead is way better than living under the same roof as you two. From the day I came back from the hospital, neither one of you understood what I've been going through."

Vickie looked insulted. "That's not fair. Both of us, in our own way, have reached out to you. But you've refused to talk to us." Her voice began to tremble as she held back tears. "I just don't understand. Things were going so well this summer. We were starting to feel like a real family."

Tessa smirked. "Gee, I wonder what happened at the end of this summer to change my mood? Hmm...let me think."

"You act like you're the only person who's ever suffered in life," Mel said. "You don't know what I've been through in my life, what Vickie's been through."

"I don't need to listen to this. You're *not* my dad!"

Vickie exploded. "I've heard enough! You're grounded. *Indefinitely.* Get inside!"

She'd never seen Vickie so angry. Fact was, she'd never seen Vickie angry at all.

"Oh, fuck off, Vickie!" Tessa pushed Vickie out of her way and charged toward the front door....

But then something stopped her....

Pain.

Excruciating pain, centered in her chest.

Tessa tried to take a gulp of air, but her lungs were frozen, unable to inflate. Her heart was a jackhammer, tearing up her insides, currents of agony radiating through every nerve in her body. Tessa cried out in horror. "Oh God!"

The lawn cushioned her fall. She could feel wet blades of grass tickling the back of her neck and could hear Vickie frantically screaming into her phone, begging them to send an ambulance right away.

Mel scooped Tessa into his arms, cradling her inert body like a wounded animal. She could see his mouth moving, but she couldn't hear him anymore.

His face was the last thing Tessa saw before darkness swallowed her up.

seven
days
before

THE HIGHLIGHT OF SHANNON'S HOUSE WASN'T THE FOUR-CAR garage, the marbled living room floor, or her parents' bedroom, which had separate his-and-hers bathrooms. It was the backyard. Shannon's backyard was like something out of a reality show. Every single detail, every single accent and color and light fixture, had been curated to impress.

The centerpiece was a kidney-shaped pool, whose thunderous waterfalls hid a secret grotto with its own screening room. Adjacent to the pool stood the outdoor kitchen cabana, which had a full-service bar and a dome-shaped pizza oven built with stone imported from Italy. The pièce de résistance was the private dock. Once you keyed yourself through the gate, you could walk down the wooden planks to the water's edge. It was here, in this idyllic spot, where you could admire the family's forty-foot catamaran, christened the *Yeo-reum*, which meant *summer* in Korean.

Despite all this abundant luxury, Shannon's family still took an annual end-of-summer vacation. Thankfully, this year, Shannon had avoided the trip by telling her parents she needed to study for her SATs. That meant Shannon would be alone in her house for nine days. Six of those days would be devoted to preparing for a balls-out party. One of those days would be for the party itself. And the final two days would be for cleanup.

Tessa helped with the planning. She ran errands with Shannon, bought cases of soda, plastic cups, chips and salsa, bottled water, limes, and margarita mix. They didn't need to buy alcohol because the outdoor bar was already stocked with liquor and Korean beer, and since Shannon's parents never hung out by the pool, they'd never realize some of it went missing.

By sundown that Saturday, familiar faces began arriving in Shannon's backyard. Within an hour, the place was packed and there were so many people talking and shouting that Shannon had to crank up the volume on the outdoor stereo system.

Tessa tried her best to make small talk with acquaintances from school, but her eyes kept wandering the crowd for Skylar. Earlier that day, he'd warned her he might be late. His grandfather had a medical scare that morning. It turned out to be a false alarm, but Skylar wanted to make certain Mike was sleeping comfortably before he left for the party.

Thank God she and Skylar were on speaking terms again.

Only a week earlier, Tessa was still worried they'd never see or talk to each other again. But then Skylar had surprised her with a call from Princeton to catch up. Tessa immediately offered him an apology for the art gallery debacle.

"I don't know what happened," she said. "I just...lost my shit. I guess I've got to work on some things."

"We all do," Skylar said sympathetically.

She felt much better after the call but wouldn't feel settled until she saw him in person. She needed to look him in the eyes when she told him she loved him—and that she had applied to RISD so they could be together after she graduated.

It was almost ten and Tessa felt buzzed from the soju. It was an odorless, tasteless liquor from Korea that packed a punch. After a single cup, she was already feeling woozy, her skin hot and moist in the humid air. She decided to get some ice for her cup. It would dilute the liquor and also cool her down. She meandered through the crowd toward the cabana but froze when she heard Skylar's voice cut through the noise. "Tessa!"

She saw him standing on the other side of the pool. He was wearing knee-length shorts and a Hawaiian shirt that was unbuttoned halfway down, revealing his tan chest. Tessa felt a flutter inside. All those days apart had only increased her desire for him. Skylar smiled and moved toward her. He'd only taken a few steps when a group of his rowing buddies, all of them blitzed, accosted him. Skylar frowned to Tessa, his expression saying: *Sorry, I'm stuck.* Tessa pointed to her cup of soju, asking: *Do you want one?* Skylar smiled. *Thank you.*

Just then, Tessa felt someone bump into her from behind. She spun around and found Shannon, unsteady on her feet, hopelessly drunk.

"I should have known all along," Shannon slurred.

Tessa was puzzled. "Known? Known what?"

"His summer job was at Sephora. *Sephora!*"

"What the hell are you talking about, Shan?"

Shannon pointed to the waterfall. Beneath it, Tessa saw Shannon's summer crush, Judd. Water was cascading down his athletic body. But that wasn't what surprised Tessa. What surprised her was that Judd had another guy in his arms and they were kissing.

"It took dating me for Judd to realize *his truth*," Shannon complained.

"Ah jeez, Shan, that totally blows. I'm really sorry."

Shannon reached for Tessa's cup of soju, desperate for another gulp. But Tessa pulled it away from her.

"Nope," Tessa said. "I'm cutting you off."

Shannon stood in place, her face the color of a cooked eggplant. She was now halfway between consciousness and that special locale called "blackout." Tessa needed to make an executive decision before her friend face-planted in the middle of her own party.

Tessa helped Shannon to her upstairs bedroom. Even here, with the windows closed, the thumping beat of hip-hop was deafening. Tessa lowered her friend into bed, then draped her beneath her thousand-thread-count duvet.

"Get some sleep, Mama," Tessa said, turning to leave. But Shannon grabbed her wrist and stopped her.

"Tessa?" Her voice sounded needy, like a little girl begging Mommy to read her a bedtime story.

"Yeah, babe?"

"You think I'll ever find someone as great as Skylar?"

Tessa smirked. "Um, doubt it."

They both giggled.

"He really sees you, doesn't he?" Shannon asked.

"It's more than that. He helps me see myself...what I am. What I could be."

"I'm still your bae, though. Right?"

Tessa swept Shannon's bangs away from her forehead and smiled warmly. "Forever and eva."

Outside, the party was still going strong. Tessa returned to the bar and poured two more cups of soju—one for her, one for Skylar. She looped around the pool and crossed onto the grassy area near the dock. She found Skylar where she'd last seen him, still surrounded by a bunch of his rowing bros. When he saw Tessa approaching, his eyes lit up. He clenched his hand and fist-bumped the guys encircling him. Then he rushed over to Tessa and pulled her into his arms.

She felt his body against hers, the sweat on his chest clinging to her clothes. The pit of unease that had been residing in Tessa's stomach since the art gallery evaporated, replaced by an overflowing happiness. It amazed her how his touch could make everything okay. Skylar lifted Tessa's chin and kissed her softly on the lips. "Hey."

"Hey back," she said, then handed Skylar his soju. He tapped the rim of his plastic cup to hers, then took a sip and kissed her once more. She could taste the sweet, bitter liquid lingering on his lips.

"Sky? Is it cool if we talk for a sec? Alone?"

"You're not still mad at me, are you," he asked.

"Not at all. I'm totally fine. I just...need to tell you something."

Tessa tugged Skylar toward the gate to the dock. She knew the entry code for the lock and planned on leading him onto Shannon's catamaran. It would be there, lying together on the water's edge, that she'd tell Skylar she loved him. But as Tessa typed the code into the keypad, a familiar voice shouted out: "Yo, brutha! I heard the good news!"

Cortez appeared behind them. He was, unsurprisingly, shirtless, his pecs covered with several fresh tattoos, though it was too dark to make any of them out.

"News?" Tessa asked. "What news?"

Skylar tensed, and his face suddenly drained of color. "Nothing's official yet," he said.

"Bullshit, bro! I spoke to Coach this morning. He said it's as good as done!"

With that, Cortez pulled the Oregon State cap off his head and squeezed it onto Skylar's. "Welcome to Oregon State, yo!"

Oregon State?

On the other side of the country?

She saw Skylar's guilty expression. "I was gonna tell you, Tess, I swear."

In her whole life, Tessa had never felt as hurt as she did in that moment. Even after being abandoned by her parents— and years of abusive foster homes—none of that came close to this feeling of betrayal. She needed to leave. She needed to leave before she detonated like a bomb that sent her heart hurtling through the air like deadly shrapnel. So she took off, pushing through the blur of faces in the crowd. She heard Skylar calling out after her. "Tessa, wait!" But she kept running, through the all-white living room and out the front door.

It wasn't until she made it onto Bayshore Drive that Skylar caught up to her. "I was gonna tell you, Tessa!" he yelled.

"When? *After* I got into RISD?"

"Of course not! I just didn't want to give you an excuse to back out. You're an amazing artist, Tessa. You belong in the best art school, no matter where I am."

"What about our plan? Same city, no more ticking clock?"

"You wouldn't even send in an application!"

"I applied last week!"

She expected this news to surprise him, but her revelation made him angrier. "Thanks for waiting until the last possible minute to tell me."

Silence. Tessa could hear the crickets, the din of the party, and the distant vibration of bass trembling through the air.

They were at a standoff. She didn't want to leave, but what else could she do?

Skylar took a deep breath. "Tessa, the truth is, my dad... he's not doing well. He's really lonely in Oregon, and I think it's best I stay with him for a while."

"Oregon's on the whole other side of the country. How will we see each other?"

"It'll be hard," he said bleakly. "But I'm *not* switching schools. I'm just deferring Brown for a year. If you get into RISD—and you will—I'll be in Providence before you are."

Tessa shook her head skeptically. "What if you like it in Oregon? Or your team starts winning? Be honest, Sky—you're just gonna up and leave?"

"Tess, my dad needs me. He's my family. You don't understand about family because..." Skylar caught himself and trailed off.

But Tessa knew what he was going to say and finished the sentence for him. "Because I never had one?"

"I'm sorry. That came out wrong."

"I *knew* this was gonna happen," Tessa said, her voice quivering. "You get close to people and all they end up doing is hurting you."

Skylar reached for her, but she stepped back, recoiling. She saw a flash of anger in his eyes. "So now you're gonna push me away like everyone else?"

Tessa was surprised at how easily the next words came out of her mouth. "The summer's over, Skylar... and so are we."

Then she turned. And ran. Her ankles and knees began to throb, but the pain felt good. Strangely, her mind turned back...back to the first conversation she'd had with Skylar, months earlier, in the movie theater. *The best love stories*, she recalled saying, *always end sadly.*

Tessa hated being right.

thirty-
nine
days
after

ONE DAY LEFT.

Tessa smelled Jasmine's perfume. That was how she knew she was back in the hospital. When her eyes lifted, she saw her favorite nurse hovering over her. She'd just punctured Tessa's vein with an IV needle and was taping the cannula to her wrist. Upon seeing Tessa awake, Jasmine shook her head disapprovingly. "Girl, didn't I warn you to take it easy?"

Dr. Nagash appeared at Tessa's bedside. He flashed a penlight into her eyes, then listened to her heartbeat with his stethoscope. His attitude, as always, was emotionless. Mel and Vickie stood behind him, wearing identical expressions of concern.

"Wh-what...h-happened?" Tessa asked.

"What happened?" Dr. Nagash repeated. "Exactly what I warned you about, Tessa. You ruptured the suture."

"How bad is it?" Vickie asked.

"The scan shows a fair amount of blood accumulated around her heart."

Mel chimed in. "Is it any wonder, the way she's been acting? Barely eating, sleeping during the day. It was only a matter of time."

Vickie admonished him. "Not now, Mel." Then she turned back to Dr. Nagash. "Is she going to be okay?"

"Not until I can drain the chamber and reinforce the original repair."

"You have to operate?" Mel said. *"Again?"*

"Unfortunately, her heart won't heal itself. We'll need to schedule her for surgery first thing tomorrow morning."

Panicked, Tessa protested. "No! I can't stay here!" She struggled to lift herself up, but Mel quickly grabbed her shoulders and pressed her back onto the bed. "You need to stay put, Tessa."

"Mel's right," Dr. Nagash said. "If I send you home, you won't make it through the night. For now, I just want you to get some rest."

Dr. Nagash spun the control wheel on Tessa's IV tube, instantly filling Tessa's body with a pleasurable lightness. "Next time you wake up, everything will be fixed."

"You don't understand...," Tessa said, her voice a whimper now. "It's...the l-last...d-day...."

Vickie looked puzzled. "The last day? The last day for what?"

But Tessa couldn't answer.

Tessa felt a cold rush of air and sensed she was moving. *They're wheeling me into the OR*, she thought. Which meant it was morning and the deadline had passed. Skylar's intermissive period had ended. He had left the bardo. There would be no more reunions, no more chances to touch him, to kiss him, to say a proper goodbye.

Tessa willed her eyes open. Her vision was blurry from the medication, but she could see she was traveling forward very quickly. She was not lying on a gurney but sitting upright in a wheelchair, which was being pushed down the hospital corridor. The hallways were desolate, which indicated it was late at night. That was odd—her surgery was scheduled for the morning, wasn't it?

Tessa held up her wrist and noticed the IV had been removed. A Band-Aid had been placed haphazardly over the puncture wound. "Jazz?" Tessa said. "Where are you taking me?"

But it wasn't Jasmine who answered Tessa. It was Shannon. "To Skylar," she said.

They came to an abrupt stop in front of the elevator banks. Shannon stepped out from behind the wheelchair and pressed the *Down* button. She turned to Tessa, her chest puffed out with pride. "Who's your bae?"

Tessa felt a swell of love for Shannon. "You are."

As they waited for the elevator to arrive, Shannon's eyes scanned the hallways for nurses or security guards who might start asking questions. After all, Tessa was a minor, so only Vickie or Mel could authorize her release. That meant the hospital could legally detain her if they wanted. But first, they'd have to catch her.

Ping! The elevator doors opened, welcoming Tessa and Shannon into the empty cube. Inside, Shannon pressed the *Lobby* button multiple times, and the doors finally slid closed.

"How did you know where I was?" Tessa asked.

"Your dead boyfriend told me."

"What?"

"Get this: I was home tonight, waiting to watch *The Bachelor.* And then I start to hear Waffles barking in my bedroom. And I mean, like, feral werewolf barking. So I go upstairs to check on him and—" Shannon stopped. "Remember the planchette? The one we used to try to contact Skylar? It was moving, without my even touching it! And when it was done, here's what I found...."

Shannon removed a sheet of paper from her pocket, unfolded it, and held it out for Tessa. She immediately recognized the distinct curves of Skylar's handwriting.

get tessa from the hospital

"I called Vickie right away, and she told me you were here, so I came as fast as I could."

"You rock, Shannon."

"Okay, so what now? Where do we go?"

"To the lake."

"You mean where he told you he loved you?"

Tessa nodded. "It's the last place on my list. That's where we'll be able to reunite—I'm sure of it."

The elevator doors opened. Shannon shoved the wheelchair forward, pushing Tessa through the barren lobby and through the automatic sliding doors. Outside, the brisk air awakened Tessa's senses, and her vision finally cleared.

Shannon stopped at the curb of the loading zone, where she'd parked her car. "Upsy-daisy," she said, hoisting Tessa to her feet.

Tessa was still weak from the meds and needed to be helped into the passenger seat. Just then, Tessa heard the lobby doors whoosh open, followed by the distinctive squawk of a walkie-talkie. Over Shannon's shoulder, she spotted two security guards running toward them. One of them called out, "Hold it right there!"

"Go, go, go!" Tessa said.

There was no time for Shannon to run around the car, so she leaped over Tessa's legs and landed in the driver's seat. Tessa yanked the door shut as Shannon started the engine. The tires made a frightful screeching sound. The car was motionless for a moment, its wheels spinning wildly. Then rubber met asphalt, and the Hyundai leaped out of the loading zone like a frenzied thoroughbred.

One of the security guards managed to catch up to the car. He was running alongside it now, grabbing the locked door handle. "Stop!" he shouted as he pounded on the passenger window with his fists.

"Hey, asshole!" Shannon screamed, offended that this rent-a-cop had dared touch her precious Hyundai. "Hands off my ride!" But by now, the guard was in the rearview mirror, a tiny action figure receding in the distance.

Exiting the hospital's driveway, Shannon made a sharp right turn. The rear half of the car fishtailed wildly before she managed to regain control. Now they were heading south on Atlantic Avenue, the opposite direction of where they needed to go.

"Wait a sec," Tessa said. "You're going the wrong way! The lake's in the other direction!"

"I know!" Shannon said.

"Well then, what are you doing? Turn around!"

Shannon tried to wrench the steering wheel to the left, but it wouldn't budge. "I can't!"

"What do you mean, you can't?"

Shannon looked nauseous. "I mean, the car's *driving itself*!"

It only took a moment for Tessa to understand what was happening. "Let it go," she ordered.

"What?"

"Let go of the wheel! Skylar's taking us someplace!"

Shannon took a deep breath and reluctantly unclenched the steering wheel. Instantly, the engine roared and the Hyundai rocketed off like a self-driving car on steroids.

"I just want you to know," Shannon said, "that I'm missing *The Bachelor* for this."

TESSA STOOD BEHIND THE REGISTER AT JACKPOT GIFTS, WATCH-
ing fat raindrops ricochet off the Boardwalk's slats. In the distance, dark clouds hung low over a stew of churning seawater.

There was something appropriate about the gloomy scene
before her. If Tessa was going to mourn the demise of her first
relationship, this was the right weather for it. It was as if her
emotional state were being projected onto nature.

Tessa was in an abyss, the abyss she'd feared was awaiting
her when she first met Skylar. And in a way, she didn't mind
being there. This was what life was all about. Accepting that,
in the end, everything turned bad. It was the story of life. At
least, it was the story of *Tessa's* life.

Skylar had sent her dozens of texts and emails and even
left several voice messages. But Tessa deleted every single one

before reading or listening to them. She did not want to hear his voice, read his words, or talk to him about anything. She had cut herself off. Now she just needed to forget the memories and move on.

Tessa suddenly noticed a customer standing across from her, on the other side of the counter. They were dressed in a rain poncho, a hood pulled up over their head, shrouding their face.

"Can I help you?" Tessa asked.

The person reached up and lowered the hood. It was Shannon. Her face was pink from exertion and she was out of breath from dashing through the rain. "Good God!" she said. "It's like a biblical plague out there!" Shannon shook out her hair, releasing a cascade of droplets that struck Tessa's face, causing her to flinch.

"What are you doing here?" Tessa asked.

"I believe the police refer to it as a mental wellness check?"

Tessa rolled her eyes and stepped out from behind the register. She crossed the store and opened the flaps of a brown box. Inside, there were dozens of bagged T-shirts with the words *Greetings from Atlantic City* printed on them. Tessa began tearing the T-shirts out of their bags and stacking them neatly on top of one another. Dull work for a dull day.

Shannon appeared behind her, like a shadow that Tessa could not escape. "Skylar told me he left you a ton of messages."

"So?"

"*So?* Tessa, you don't ghost your soul mate!"

Tessa didn't reply. She continued unbagging the T-shirts.

"This is a *seriously* messed-up way of proving a point," Shannon said.

"What point?"

"You always say there's no such thing as happy endings. And now you're screwing up an amazing relationship just to prove it?"

"Shannon, I know you came here to help. And I appreciate that. But you can't help me. No one can help. Because I'll *never* be the girl who Skylar needs me to be. My past, who I am, everything that's happened to me—it's always going to get in the way."

Seemingly at her breaking point, Shannon kicked the box of T-shirts with ferocity, propelling it down the aisle.

"What the hell!" Tessa said.

"Remember last spring…when we cut school and drove up to Philly to go shopping?"

"I don't want to hear this—"

"Only, on the way up, you spotted that condemned bridge that you just *had* to get some photos of? But not normal photos. No, Tessa Jacobs needed to dive into the river below the bridge in order to get *the perfect shot*. Did it matter that she didn't have a bathing suit? No. Did it matter that the water was freezing cold and was filled with, like, ectoplasmic waste? No."

"Get to the point, Shannon."

"When I saw you down there, swimming against the

currents with your camera, you know what I was thinking? I was thinking...just imagine if Tessa could take risks like this for her life and not just for her art."

In that moment, something clicked inside Tessa. Shannon was right. Tessa had always bragged that she'd do anything to take a great photo, even risk her own life. Why couldn't she apply that same risk-taking spirit to her relationship with Skylar? Wasn't he worth it?

"He's leaving tonight," Shannon said. "You need to talk to him before he does."

Shannon flipped the poncho's hood back over her head. Tessa watched her walk to the front of the store, then stop, peering out at the downpour, tentative.

Tessa felt a sudden, urgent need to see Skylar. She realized she couldn't let him leave without talking to him. It was probably too late to repair things, but that didn't matter. She needed to take a chance. Once and for all, she needed to tame the frightened little girl inside her.

Tessa blurted out, "Shannon, wait!" She rushed to her friend's side, stopping her from leaving. Tessa gestured to the empty store behind them. "Will you take over for me?"

"You can't be serious."

"Please. I can't leave unless someone's behind the register," Tessa said.

"Babe, you know I don't do the minimum-wage thing...." Shannon grinned. "But for you, I'll make an exception."

•

Tessa pressed the buzzer on the wall. A loud *ding* echoed through the bus, indicating that Tessa's stop was next. She stood up and rushed down the aisle. The floor beneath her was slick with rainwater, and in order not to slip, she had to grasp the seat backs as she moved to the front of the bus. The driver noticed Tessa standing beside him and hit the brakes. "Cover up," he said. "It's nasty out there."

Nodding, Tessa reached into her backpack, looking for her hoodie, but she hadn't brought it to work that day. Then she noticed something hidden in the depths of her backpack....

It was Skylar's orange hat.

Once again, without her realizing it, Skylar had snuck it back into her bag, a sweet reminder that he was never too far from her. Seeing it warmed her heart.

Tessa pulled the hat out and slipped it over her head. The bus came to a stop and the doors folded open. When Tessa stepped from the bus, her feet landed in an ankle-high puddle of rainwater. She instantly felt the wetness seeping through her canvas sneakers. She was drenched but didn't care. She needed to get to Skylar. It was past eight now, and she could only pray he hadn't left already.

Tessa began to run, her feet splashing the rivers of water that were rushing along the sidewalks. Her lungs began to burn for oxygen, but she remembered what Skylar had taught her about physical pain: *Make it your friend.* So Tessa kept running, embracing the discomfort.

When she turned the corner onto Douglas Avenue, Tessa saw red taillights glowing within the downpour. It was Skylar's jeep. He had just backed out of his grandfather's driveway. He was leaving—at that exact moment.

Frantic, Tessa screamed: "Skylar!" But the rain drowned out her voice. She began running toward the rear of his jeep, screaming louder. "SKYLAR! WAIT!"

But the jeep took off, heading down the street.

Tessa fumbled in her back pocket for her phone. It slipped from her grasp and splashed into a deep puddle on the street. Retrieving it from beneath the water, she saw its screen was dark; the phone was dead. "Shit!"

She looked up again and saw Skylar's jeep turning the corner. She had only one chance now—she had to cut Skylar off on the next street over.

She sprang onto the sidewalk and ran across the mushy lawn of a neighboring house. She heaved garbage pails out of her way, hurdled over a wooden fence, and landed on the sticky mud. She dashed through the adjoining backyard and onto their driveway, then charged into the street and stopped at the center of North Clermont Avenue.

Up ahead, she could see Skylar's jeep. Tessa looked up. The streetlamp above her was broken, its flickering bulb a dim ember of light. Tessa was now couched in a pool of darkness, hidden behind sheets of rain.

Skylar's jeep was racing directly at her, his headlights growing in size. Tessa felt rising fear spreading through her body. "Skylar!" she screamed. "Skylar, stop!"

But his jeep didn't slow down.

forty
days
after

SHANNON'S CAR CAME TO A SCREECHING STOP. THE ENGINE shut itself off and the parking brake depressed on its own. Tessa and Shannon breathed a sigh of relief. It wasn't every day that a disembodied spirit chauffeured you around.

They glanced through the windshield. They were on a residential street in Margate, lined by houses on both sides.

Shannon was baffled. "Why did he take us . . . *here*?"

"You've completely forgotten, haven't you?" Tessa replied.

"Forgotten what?"

Tessa tried to jog her friend's memory. "Look around you. We're on North Clermont Avenue." But Shannon was still puzzled. "Shannon! This is the last place I saw Skylar. It's where the accident happened!"

Shannon's eyes swelled with recognition. "Yassssssss."

Up until that moment, Tessa had deliberately avoided the accident scene. She wouldn't even drive past it, though a few times she'd considered going to light a candle or lay some flowers. But she always decided she couldn't handle it. She'd lost more than Skylar in this spot. She'd lost the best part of herself.

"I don't get it," Shannon said. "Didn't Doris say you were supposed to go to the places you felt *closest*? How could you feel close *here*, in the spot where you both, like, croaked?"

"I don't know. But I'm going to find out."

As Tessa reached for the door handle, Shannon grabbed her shoulder. "You want me to come along? Just in case?"

Tessa smiled with affection. "You're an amazing friend, Shan. But I'm pretty sure you don't have a ticket to where I'm going."

Shannon nodded with regret. "In that case," she said, "I'll just...wait here?"

"Good plan," Tessa said.

Stepping out of the car, Tessa felt a cold blast of wind across her face. As she walked to the middle of the street, she saw shriveled leaves tumbling over one another, scratching the pavement as if escaping an invisible enemy.

Despite standing at the scene of the accident, Tessa was unable to recall anything about what had happened that night. In Hollywood movies, when a hero with amnesia returned to the scene of the crime, all their memories conveniently flooded back. Sadly, Tessa's mind was still a blank.

She heard buzzing. Tessa looked up and saw a broken streetlamp, the filament inside its bulb struggling to produce a wisp of light. It was one of the few things Tessa could recall about that night. The streetlight, flickering on and off like a strobe. All these months later, they still hadn't fixed it.

Tessa wondered why she didn't feel Skylar's presence around her. He must be near; he'd driven her to this spot. She called out to him. "Sky?"

At first, the shift was subconscious. It was hard to pinpoint exactly what was changing around her until Tessa noticed that everything was dimming. She fixed her gaze on the house across the street from her. Its front lawn was illuminated by dozens of landscape lights. All of them were fading in unison, as if the electricity was being siphoned off. It was the same with every house on the block. Inside and outside, all their lights were going dark.

The streetlamp above her began to surge with golden-white light. Somehow, all the energy draining from the neighborhood was channeling into this single bulb.

Tessa was suddenly enveloped in a blanket of warmth. Her insides were swirling. It was like the first dip of a roller coaster, a cataclysmic rush of euphoria and fear. She had the pronounced feeling that she was dissolving, particle by particle. She lifted her hand in front of her eyes and was startled to discover she was translucent. Tessa's fingers were vanishing, while at the same time, the world around her was receding. It was like watching a photograph being developed, only in reverse. The contours of everything on the street were disappearing—the color, the light, all of it evaporating from her sensory experience.

Then she heard a loud, concussive *pop*. Overhead, the light bulb exploded. A fountain of sparks cascaded down over Tessa like a waterfall of glittering confetti. The last thing she heard before everything went white was Shannon's voice screaming out her name.

the
in
between

WHAT?

Why am I in . . . the Little Art Theater?

Tessa was sitting in her usual seat, disoriented. Somehow, she'd been teleported from the street, but the phenomenon responsible for moving her hadn't sent her very far. At most, she was a mile away from the crash scene.

Is this a dream?

Am I in surgery, imagining this?

Why am I . . . here?

As if answering her unspoken questions, the lights faded, and the white screen came to life. A movie was now being projected onto it. But not just any movie. It wasn't a comedy or a drama or an action film. It was Tessa's life—the final moments leading up to the accident. The final moments that, no matter how hard she tried, she could never remember.

Tessa saw herself standing in the middle of North Clermont Avenue. It was raining hard, and her hair was hanging over her face like a tangled mop. Down the street, Skylar's jeep was speeding toward her. He didn't see her. The street was too dark, his headlights no match for the torrent of rain. On-screen, Tessa cried out: "Skylar, stop!" But his jeep kept bearing down on her, like an animal hunting its prey. Suddenly, the flickering streetlamp spontaneously flashed on, and Tessa's figure flushed with light.

Skylar's tires abruptly locked in place, sending up sheets of mist. He'd seen her. The jeep hydroplaned across the slick pavement, an out-of-control metal monster careering toward Tessa. Finally, his swirling tires gripped the concrete, and the jeep came to a staggered stop just a few yards from her. The headlights blinked off, and after a moment, the driver's side door swung open. Skylar stepped out of his jeep. "Tess?"

On the street, Tessa smiled wistfully and pulled the orange cap off her head. She held it out for him. "You forgot your hat."

Tessa was crying now, but there was no way to tell, because her tears were mixing with the rivers of rain spilling down her face. She walked toward Skylar and took his hand in hers. "I'm so sorry, Sky."

He shook his head. "No. *I'm* the one who needs to apologize. I should have talked to you first, before I made any decision about college."

"You shouldn't have to explain loving your family....If I hadn't spent my whole life pushing people away, I would have understood that."

In the theater, Tessa felt uneasy. As much as she wanted to see what had transpired that night, she worried about violating the privacy of these two people. It made no sense. She was watching herself and Skylar, yet why did it feel like she was spying on them? The scene playing on the screen suddenly froze. It was as if Tessa's misgivings had paused the movie. But it was too late for Tessa to turn away. Her curiosity had reached a fever pitch. She needed to see the rest of the scene. And as soon as that desire circulated through her mind, the film magically resumed playing.

"You're soaking wet," Skylar said. "Come back to my jeep."

He clasped Tessa's hand and tried to pull her toward his jeep, but Tessa stood in place. Skylar turned back to her, confused. "What's wrong?"

"I love you," Tessa said.

Sitting in the dark theater, Tessa felt an electric shock of surprise. *I said it!*

Since Skylar's death, Tessa's greatest fear was that her final interaction with him had been a bad one. Even worse was the belief that she'd never reciprocated his declaration of love. Now she knew that wasn't true. She *had* said the words. That girl up there—the one who'd opened her heart—she wanted to be that girl again.

Back on the screen, Skylar was moved. He clenched his jaw, as if embarrassed to reveal the effect her words had on him.

"Would you mind," Tessa asked, "if I said it again?"

Her simple question broke Skylar's armor, and he began to cry. "No," he said. "I wouldn't mind."

This time, Tessa told him in French. She had secretly taught herself the words. "*Je t'aime*," she said.

"*Je t'aime aussi*," he replied through tears.

As the rain beat down on them, they kissed. A kiss so powerful that it mended their hearts, replacing weeks of uncertainty and anxiety with the wholeness of true love. With their eyes closed, neither Tessa nor Skylar noticed the streetlight above them blinking off. They were now two figures, sewn together, cloaked in darkness. Still kissing, they did not see the flare of headlights from behind Skylar's jeep, nor did they hear the sound of the approaching car in the deafening rain.

From her seat in the theater, Tessa saw what was coming. She covered her mouth in horror and cried out, "NO!"

As if the characters on-screen had heard her, Skylar and Tessa broke their kiss and turned toward the oncoming lights. Then came the nauseating, crunching sound of impact. Instantly, Skylar's jeep catapulted off the street. Two tons of metal, now airborne, were hurtling directly toward them. There was only enough time for Skylar to spin his back to the jeep and protect Tessa from the brunt of the impact. The last thing he saw—his final glimpse—was the face of the girl he loved, the girl he now knew loved him back.

In the theater, Tessa could not bear to watch what came next, and strangely, once again, the movie followed her mental commands. The screen went dim and the lights rose up.

Tessa was frozen in her seat, absorbing what she'd just seen. What was it that Charles Dickens had written? *It was the best of times; it was the worst of times....* Yes. That perfectly encapsulated what she'd just witnessed. Tessa had overcome her greatest fear in life—she had opened her heart. Mere seconds later, the universe had delivered a brutal twist of fate and taken away the boy who'd helped open it.

It was then that Tessa realized she was gripping something. And it wasn't the armrest. She was clutching something... warm. It felt like... human flesh.

It felt like an arm.

She slowly turned. Her throat seized up with inexpressible joy and awe. Because now, sitting next to her in the Little Art Theater was Skylar.

Alive.

Overwhelmed by his physical presence, Tessa could only muster a single word. "Y-you?"

Skylar flashed a serene smile and nodded. "Me."

"No halos? Or wings?"

"Just me," he said.

Weeks of yearning exploded from within her. She shrieked and dove into Skylar's arms, holding him, feeling him, inhaling his familiar scent. It was like a thirst that could not be quenched, even by an ocean of water. She couldn't tell how long they were holding each other. She just knew that the boy she loved was in her arms and she never wanted to let go.

"I was starting to worry you wouldn't make it in time," he said.

"You didn't exactly make it easy!" she said, pulling back to look at him.

"Sorry about that," he said. "It's kind of like...you guys are riding on bicycles while we're flying jets. Slowing down to interact, even for a few seconds, takes a lot of practice."

Wiping her tears, Tessa looked around and gestured at their surroundings. "So this is it? The bardo is...a movie theater?"

"Not exactly," he said. "Come on."

Skylar grabbed Tessa's hand and tugged her up the aisle and through the theater's exit. Outside on the sidewalk, they were still in the town of Margate. It was midday, and everything looked the way it always did.

"We're home? In Margate?" Tessa asked.

"It's not the Margate you think. Everything you see is a thought form."

"A what?"

"A thought form. It's like...a combination of your memory and your imagination. What you can't remember, your mind creates and fills in."

Tessa turned back to the street before her, suddenly

cognizant that it wasn't inhabited. There were no people on the sidewalks, no cars on Ventnor Avenue.

"Okay, so . . . where is everyone?"

"Try thinking about them."

"People, you mean?"

"Yeah. Think about . . . people driving their cars."

The instant Tessa thought about moving cars, they appeared, cruising down the street like any other day in Margate. From her mind to reality in the blink of an eye.

"Holy crap!" Tessa shrieked.

"Pretty awesome, right?"

Tessa immediately considered the implications of her new-found superpower. "What if I think of something that *doesn't* exist?"

"Like what?" Skylar asked.

"I don't know. What if I think of . . . purple rain?"

Suddenly, Tessa felt warm drops striking her body. She looked up and saw a deluge of purple rain falling from a cloudless sky. Elated, she jumped up and down like a little kid who'd just received her dream Christmas present. Then she covered Skylar's face with a flurry of kisses. "Don't make me leave."

"Let's not worry about that right now," he said reassuringly. "Just tell me what you want to do."

"Be with you."

"You are with me. . . . Where do you want to go?"

"I don't care."

Skylar flashed a conspiratorial smile.

"What?" Tessa asked, intrigued.

"I've got an idea."

Suddenly, the world around them—the streets, the cars, the people—evaporated. When Tessa looked away from Skylar's eyes, she found she was no longer in Margate.

I'm in Paris! As in Paris, France.

They were on a quaint street in the Left Bank. There was a busy outdoor café, a fruit stand on wheels, and an adorable little pastry shop, its window filled with immaculate rows of French confections. Everything Tessa saw was in vibrant Technicolor.

When the reality of where she was set in, Tessa cried out. *"Mon dieu! C'est incredible!"*

Wait a second. She was speaking fluent French; how was that possible? She turned to Skylar, but he anticipated her question.

"Yes. You can speak any language you want here," he said in French.

"Comment est mon accent?" Tessa said.

"Your accent's perfect," he replied.

Once again, Tessa surveyed the street before her. She felt a bubble of inspiration floating up. "Would it be all right if I . . . tweaked it a little?"

"Be my guest."

Tessa's mind wound back to the myriad of photographs that had hung over her bed. The photos, most of them by Brassaï, depicted Paris in the 1930s and '40s. It was the glamorous Paris that Tessa yearned to see but knew she never could. The past, as they often said, was past. But here, Tessa was limited only by what her mind could conjure.

Relying on her memory of those photos, Tessa began to transform the street, turning back time. Modern SUVs morphed into vintage Renaults. Concrete sidewalks changed into cobblestone streets. Every detail she remembered from the photos was materializing before her. Even people's clothes changed. At the café now, men were wearing suits and fedoras, the women pleated skirts and cashmere wraps.

It needs to be night. The sky darkened.

It needs to be foggy. The mist formed.

She thought of scooters, the kind that used to fill the streets of all the great European cities. Before she could blink, an old Vespa swept past, leaving her and Skylar in a cloud of diesel exhaust.

Like an artist contemplating her latest canvas, Tessa stepped back to consider her work. She was pleased with her changes but sensed an element was missing.

"Aren't you forgetting something?" Skylar asked.

Forgetting something? What had she missed?

Skylar egged her on. "Come on—it's the most important part."

It suddenly occurred to Tessa what was missing. Or rather, what *needed* to be missing. Color! The Paris depicted in all her favorite photos was in black and white. But could she actually do that?

"Try it," Skylar suggested, reading her mind.

Tessa thought back to the images, and everything around her instantly drained of color. Even she and Skylar were now in black and white! It was mind-bogglingly surreal. Tessa was no longer *looking* at a photo on her wall; she was *inside* the photo, its subject.

"Gah!" Tessa yelled.

"What's the matter?" Skylar asked.

"You didn't tell me to bring my camera!"

They walked along the river Seine, hand in hand. Beside them, old riverboats puttered up the waterway. Tessa could hear the gaiety of the ship's passengers as they drifted by, their laughter dissolving into the warm night.

"The Buddhists call it the bardo," Skylar explained. "The Muslims, the Barzakh. Nearly every religion and culture has a name for this place. But my favorite of all is Summerland."

"And everyone comes here after they die?"

"That's right. In order to grieve."

"You mean, the dead grieve, too?" Tessa asked.

"You think only the living mourn the dead? I left behind everything. My parents, the girl I loved, not to mention a lifetime of dreams."

Selfishly caught up in her own grief, Tessa had never stopped to consider that Skylar might be mourning, too.

"It's not fair," Tessa said.

"I know it seems that way. But when you arrive here, you learn it's just one of many incarnations. All of us have lived hundreds of lives. It's a cycle with no beginning and no end." Skylar stopped walking. Tessa saw a hint of sadness in his eyes. "Tess, you probably know this already, but—"

"We don't have a lot of time?" He shook his head with regret. Tessa continued. "Well, I know where I want to go."

Skylar smiled, his expression challenging her. "Surprise me."

Tessa nodded. And conjured a place . . .

The earth beneath her feet went soft. She looked down and saw that the cobblestone had transformed into sparkling white sand. They were now on a beach. The sea behind them was impossibly green, as if lit from within. On the horizon, the golden orb of the sun was frozen in a perpetual sunset. Or was it sunrise? It didn't matter. All that mattered was that the sky looked like magic.

"You're catching on fast," Skylar said, clearly impressed.

"You haven't seen the best part," Tessa said. She pointed over his shoulder. He turned. On the sand, a few hundred feet from the water, there was a tiny beach shack on stilts. It was an exact replica of the one that Betty and Zorg had lived in together in the film *Betty Blue*.

"Is it okay?" Tessa asked.

"It's more than okay," Skylar said. "It's perfect."

•

She was not sure how long they were making love. It may have been hours; it may have been years. Time was different here. It felt like a continuous dream.

Later, they lay together, exhausted. Under the thin white sheets, they studied each other's features with desperation. Every curve and every line harbored secrets they yearned to explore.

"Have we met in the past?" Tessa asked. "Before I was Tessa and you were Skylar?"

"Many, many times," Skylar said.

"So . . . we'll meet again?"

"Many, many times."

"How will I know it's you?"

Skylar cradled her face and looked at her, his green eyes filled with love. "You'll know."

A soft breeze stirred Tessa awake. She was still in bed, wrapped in a tangle of sheets. She sensed the absence next to her and her heart jumped. Where was Skylar? She sat up, worried their time had run out, and that Skylar was gone. But she was relieved when she saw him on the outdoor deck, lounging on a wicker sofa.

Outside, the air was pleasantly cool and smelled of the sea. She sat behind him and pulled his back into her chest. She admired the horizon. It was a sunburst of colors that were physically impossible anywhere but here.

"It's so beautiful," Tessa said. "Is it a sunrise...or a sunset?"

"It's both," Skylar said, his voice melancholy. "An ending... *and* a beginning."

Tessa did not know why, but his answer made her realize that their time together was coming to an end. This magical place, this magical time, birthed by their love, was fading.

"I've spent my whole life learning how not to get hurt," Tessa said. "It's no way to live....But even with all the hurt I've experienced these past few months, I don't regret a thing. Because I love you, Sky. And knowing I can feel this way makes life worth living."

Tears sprang from Skylar's eyes. "My grandfather used to say there's a price you pay for love. And now I realize what it is....Somehow, someway...it has to end."

Tessa could now see the beach through Skylar's face. He was dissolving before her eyes.

"I love you, Tessa."

"I'll always love you," she replied. "Forever."

As they held each other, Tessa felt Skylar's palm pressing against her chest, over her scar. There was a sudden warm sensation inside. It felt like rays of love penetrating her broken heart, mending her wounds.

Skylar's last words came as a whisper, no louder than the ocean waves in the distance.

"Now go give us a happy ending," he said.

epilogue

ON SATURDAY MORNING AT TEN SHARP, TESSA KNOCKED ON Grandpa Mike's door. From inside, she heard his voice calling out to her—"Coming!"—followed by the sound of his feet shuffling across the linoleum floor. The lock clicked and his door swung open. Mike stood before her, dressed in a sweat suit, his feet buried in fur-lined moccasins.

"Right on time! Come on in, Tessa," he said brightly.

When Tessa entered the home, it was like stepping into a time machine. All those summer nights she had spent here with Skylar—reading poetry, watching old movies, and talking late into the night as they curled up close. But the rush of memories didn't make Tessa feel sad or nostalgic. Instead, she felt thankful. How lucky she was to have shared Skylar's final months on earth. That was a gift to be cherished.

Grandpa Mike turned into the living room. "She's here," he said.

Skylar's parents sat shoulder to shoulder on the sofa. There was a somber feeling in the air. Skylar's absence was like an open wound. Could a mother and father ever truly get over the loss of a child?

Leigh was clutching a damp ball of crumpled tissues. Her eyes were red and swollen. Carl looked thinner than Tessa remembered. Granted, they'd only met twice on FaceTime. But the months of mourning had undoubtedly changed his appearance. He looked older, even fragile.

"Hi," Tessa said.

Carl and Leigh rose from the sofa and embraced Tessa, one at a time. Each hug felt different. Leigh's hug transmitted yearning, as if she were trying to connect to her son through Tessa's body. Carl's hug was stronger. It was sending a wordless message: *It's going to be okay; we'll get through this.*

"I'll make some tea," Grandpa Mike said, turning into the kitchen.

Tessa found her way to a chair, and Skylar's parents returned to the sofa.

"How's your recovery going?" Carl asked. "We heard you were back in the hospital."

"Just for a few nights. It turned out to be a false alarm," Tessa said.

"Oh?" Leigh asked.

"It's a pretty crazy story, actually.... You see, the accident tore a part of my heart. And they repaired it. Only I didn't exactly follow doctor's orders and the repair ruptured.... The thing is, when they finally wheeled me into the OR and opened me up, they discovered that, somehow, my heart had healed itself."

Carl's eyes widened. "No kidding?"

"No kidding," Tessa said. "My doctor said it was the second time in the same year that I was his *miracle patient*."

"Maybe you got a little help from upstairs?" Leigh said, raising a finger toward heaven.

"For sure," Tessa said.

It was then that Leigh and Carl noticed that Tessa was holding two identically wrapped gifts. Both were rectangular and the exact same size.

"Were we supposed to bring gifts?" Carl asked.

"Actually, this was Skylar's idea," Tessa said. She crossed the room and handed one to each of them. "He planned on giving them to you for your anniversary."

Leigh choked up and began to cry. Attempting to soothe her, Carl squeezed her hand tenderly. Despite all they'd been through, Tessa could still see the love these two people shared.

Leigh wiped her eyes dry. "You first," she said, prompting her husband to open his gift.

"No," Carl said. "You go, Leigh."

She nodded and drew a breath to steel herself. Then slipped her fingers between the seams of the wrapping paper, tearing it off in jagged strips. Now Leigh was cradling a framed photo of her son. It was the picture that Tessa had taken of Skylar at Cooper River, the morning that fate had reunited them. Skylar was in his rowing shell and had just crossed the finish line. His arms were over his head in triumph. In that moment, in his expression of pure exhilaration, one could see everything that made Skylar special.

Leigh sniffled, her eyes filled with gratitude. "It's lovely, Tessa, thank you."

"Your turn, Carl," Tessa said.

Carl tore off the wrapping paper and found the same photo of Skylar in an identical frame.

"One for Leigh's house," Tessa said. "And one for yours."

Tessa saw confusion cross their faces. She realized she needed to explain it to them. "At first, it was hard for him to accept. You know Skylar—he was a dreamer, a believer in love. He felt if you guys got divorced, it would be like betraying the love you once had for each other. But he changed his mind. He told me he wanted you to be happy."

Leigh and Carl remained silent, absorbing what Tessa had just told them. Finally, Carl broke the silence. "You're certain this is what he wanted?"

"Yes," Tessa said. "It's what he told me."

"Before the accident?" Leigh asked.

Strangely, Tessa had anticipated this question. She smiled and answered. "Well, he couldn't have told me *after*, could he?"

But of course, that was exactly what Skylar had done.

●

Morning light fell onto Tessa's face. She'd awakened long before dawn, but her nervousness about the day ahead kept her in bed, suspended in thought, watching the rosy sunlight spread across her walls.

She could smell pancakes, and her stomach stirred. The night before, Tessa had forgotten to eat dinner. She needed every minute—every second—to prepare for today, and food was a needless time suck.

She dressed quickly. Jeans, cable-knit sweater, silvery flats. She slid her computer into its laptop sleeve, zipped it closed, and carried it downstairs with her.

In the kitchen, the air was thick with smoky sweetness. Vickie was at the stovetop, frying silver-dollar pancakes in a puddle of brown butter. Tessa entered and kissed her on the cheek. "Morning," Tessa said.

"Big day," Vickie replied.

"So they tell me." Ravenous, Tessa grabbed a pancake off the pile and stuffed it into her mouth. In seconds, her stomach was filled with a glutenous, spongy warmth, and her hunger pangs eased.

"Take human bites, Tessa."

"Mm...delish."

"Sit down—I'll make you a plate."

"No time. There might be traffic, and I don't want to be late."

Nodding, Vickie placed the spatula on the counter and pulled Tessa into her arms. "You're going to be great."

"Thanks, Mom."

It felt so good to use that word. Not just good but *right*. There were so many things Tessa regretted about the past, but the thing she regretted most was how she had treated Vickie. It was hard to fathom there was a time, not too long ago, when Tessa viewed her as an adversary. In fact, Vickie cared about Tessa more than any adult ever had. She was lucky to have this kind, intelligent woman in her life. And Tessa vowed to always treat her as family.

Outside, the November air was pleasantly fresh, and Tessa could smell traces of smoke from her neighbors' fireplaces. As she climbed into Vickie's SUV, she saw Mel carrying the leaf blower out of the opened garage. He was holding a half-eaten Pop-Tart in one hand, and his chin was covered with crumbs of white frosting.

"Hey, Dad? Maybe it's time to—you know—lay off the junk food?"

Mel pretended to be baffled by her question. But of course, he knew exactly what Tessa was talking about.

Tessa pulled her phone out and pointed it at Mel. "Smile." Mel forced a lopsided grin and Tessa took a snapshot of his physique. Then she waved him over so he could look at the photo.

"That's a bad angle," he insisted.

"Vickie says you can't fit into your work uniform anymore?"

"Christ, now it's two against one."

Tessa looked at Mel, sincerity in her eyes. "Mom and I really care about you."

Mel glanced at the photo again, then grunted. "Aw hell, maybe I could lose a few pounds?"

Tessa snatched the remains of the Pop-Tart from Mel's hand and started the car. Mel reached through the open window and patted her shoulder. "Good luck, kiddo."

The RISD portfolio day was being held at a local community college. Tessa had been to the campus only once before, to attend a lecture on environmental photography. But today was different. Today, the theater where she'd once been an audience member would be filled with other college applicants and, more important, the admissions committee.

For Tessa, being here was no longer about Skylar; it was about realizing the potential she knew she had but had been afraid to admit. Like a compass, Skylar had pointed the way. But now Tessa had to put the compass down and choose which path she wanted to follow. Her future, whatever it held, would be her own.

At the welcome desk, a stern, no-nonsense woman assigned Tessa a number. "Once your number is called, you'll have five minutes to set up your equipment. Your presentation cannot exceed seven minutes or your application will be null and void.... Good luck to you."

Tessa entered the crowded, noisy auditorium. There were hundreds of other students in here. *Arty types*, as Shannon affectionately called them. They had nose piercings, tattoo sleeves and dyed hair, and many were dressed in thrift-shop attire.

Tessa found a seat to the left of the aisle, with enough space between her and another girl so she wouldn't have to make small talk. As she waited for her number to be called, she watched the other students—her competition—make their presentations. There was a calming monotony to it all. The proctor would call out a number and the applicant would come up, connect their computer to the projector, then display their photos on a screen hanging on the curtain behind them. All the while, these applicants would furtively glance at the blank faces in the front row—the admissions officers. These were the gatekeepers who held their futures in their hands.

Tessa's mood changed based on the quality of the work being presented. The lesser work made her feel confident; the innovative work made her feel hopeless. In the end, she concluded that her technical skill might not be as good as some of the others, but her voice was uniquely her own. If Tessa was going to land a spot in this coveted program, it would be her way of "seeing things" that would be responsible.

She'd been sitting for more than an hour when she finally heard her number called. As Tessa walked up the steps to the stage, her heart raced, but she did not feel any pain. As Dr. Nagash had said, marveling at her recovery: "It's like the accident never even happened." But of course, Tessa knew that wasn't true. There was still the pinkish scar that ran across her chest, the scar that would forever remind her of the night everything had changed.

Tessa placed her laptop on the dais. She fumbled through the tangle of cables and connected her computer to the nearby projector. The prior week, Tessa had transcribed her entire presentation onto index cards, but she had practiced it so many times, she no longer needed them. In a way, it felt like everything that had happened in her life had led her to this moment.

She cleared her throat and began. "Ever since I was a little girl, people have told me that I see things that no one else does. And I believe this is the reason I was first drawn to photography. My camera wasn't just a way to express myself. It was the means by which I memorialized the unseen, the ephemeral.... And yet, despite my sensitivity to the unnoticed, it was only recently that I discovered something I'd been blind to...." Tessa paused for dramatic effect. "A ghost."

She clicked the arrow on her computer. A photograph appeared on the screen looming over her. It was a black-and-white still of Tessa, sitting alone in the Little Art Theater, the seat beside her empty. It was from the night she went looking for Skylar's spirit. The photo was composed in such a way that it gave the distinct feeling of *absence*. It seemed to be saying: *Someone is missing from this frame.*

Tessa continued. "All of us—each and every one of us—is haunted by ghosts. The ghosts of childhood traumas, the ghosts of unfulfilled dreams, the ghosts of lost love...

Understandably, many of us treat these ghosts as unwanted visitors. As malevolent spirits who have forced their way into our homes, taking up residence and refusing to leave."

Tessa clicked the button again. Another photo appeared. It was Tessa, all alone, in black and white. She was sitting at the picnic table at Smitty's, facing an empty seat—the seat where Skylar had once sat. It depicted emptiness and loss.

"Like most people, I believed that if I simply ignored these ghosts, they would eventually go away. This, however, turned out to be a mistake."

Another photo: this one of Tessa walking alone on the misty shoreline, a re-creation of the first photo she had taken of Skylar. Now *she* was the apparition.

"You see, like all our worst fears, these invisible spirits gain strength in the darkness. If we run from them, they run faster. If we push them away, they push back harder. How, then, can we make room for the new when we are haunted by the old?"

Tessa felt a sense of relief. She was coming to the end of her presentation.

"It has taken great personal loss for me to discover the answer to this question. We must *attend* to our ghosts. We must welcome them into our lives and embrace them because they are a *part of us*. Only when we finally acknowledge their presence will they make room for new experiences . . . and new possibilities. . . ."

Tessa's final photo was different from the rest. It was a close-up of her face. In color. She had taken it at the Empyrean

Hotel, on the night she first saw Skylar's spirit. But of the hundreds of people looking at this photo, only Tessa knew the tiny glint in her eyes was the reflection of a ghost—the ghost of a boy who loved her so much that he had crossed the boundary of life and death to be with her one last time.

"In the end, I have learned that we cannot shun our deepest selves. Our ghosts make us who we are and who we hope to be. And like the bittersweet memories of first love, we carry these hauntings inside us, tethered irrevocably to our hearts...."

Tessa smiled. "In life...in death...and everywhere in between."

Acknowledgments

For the last twenty-plus years I have made my living as a screenwriter, and screenwriters don't get to write acknowledgments. Thus, I ask your indulgence as I thank some of the people who helped bring this book to life, and a few others who've had a profound effect on my career.

On the business side, I would like to thank Jeremy Barber and Byrd Leavell at UTA for guiding the book to its home at Little, Brown Books for Young Readers. Their collective experience and wise counsel made the transition from screenwriter to novelist a seamless one.

Additional thanks are due to my longtime lawyer, Karl Austen, who's more than just a hard-nosed dealmaker. He's also Hollywood's shrewdest consigliere.

I'd like to thank Andrew Deane, Sally Ware, and Dan Spilo at Industry Entertainment, as well as Joey and Jamie King, for their help in turning what began as a partial manuscript into a movie deal, which became a screenplay, which became the book you're now holding.

Much thanks to Ali Bell, formerly of Paramount Players, for allowing me the time and space to refine the story in order to make it workable. Many in her position would have cut bait, but her patience as I struggled through the dual-timeline structure was a godsend.

Also, a quick shoutout to Pete Harris at Temple Hill, whose encouragement and guidance was extraordinarily helpful in the early days of this book.

Creatively, I would like to thank Todd Goldman for his ever-watchful set of proofreading eyes; Danny Karsevar, for providing me with his memories as a Margate lifeguard; and a special thanks to my niece, Isabel Klein, for her spot-on notes and for being my "teen whisperer."

Arie Posin, the film's director, deserves a special note of thanks. With great patience and the right amount of pressure, Arie helped me deepen and clarify the script and all its characters. Consequently, he made this book so much better than it would have been.

Special thanks are also due to my editor, Samantha Gentry, who handled this first-time novelist like the seasoned pro that she is. Her queries and thoughtful notes made the entire process, from beginning to end, a joy.

On the research front, I'd like to thank Iva Boteva, who taught me how to scull, and thus brought realism to the rowing chapters.

I am deeply indebted to Dr. Mark Plunkett, a brilliant heart surgeon, who has generously advised me on several different projects, and has always provided me with the perfect amount of medical jargon to make it all sound real.

I am personally grateful to Kirsten "Kiwi" Smith for convincing me, many years ago, to write a book. Kiwi's enthusiasm is an unstoppable runaway train. I'm glad I decided to jump on board rather than getting run over and flattened.

Special acknowledgment must be given to Robbie Brenner, a friend, compatriot, and parallel-world soul mate. Robbie makes magic with everything she touches. Her advocacy on behalf of this project—and my career as a whole—is simply impossible to quantify.

And finally, I would like to thank my parents, Howard and Paula Klein, for providing me with a loving home to grow up in and allowing my creativity to flourish. It was the sound of my father's clattering typewriter that lulled me to sleep as a young boy. All those late nights taught me the work ethic required to be a writer. Thank you, Mom and Dad. I love you very much.

John Chapple

MARC KLEIN has written the screen-plays for many well-known movies, including the romantic comedy classic *Serendipity*, as well as *Mirror, Mirror*, a reimagining of the Snow White fairy tale. *The In Between* is his debut novel and the basis for the upcoming film from Paramount Pictures. Marc resides in Los Angeles. He invites you to visit him at marckleinauthor.com or follow him on Twitter @marcsklein.